IT'S ALSO ABOUT

MYNAH

Rucha Chitrodia, a journalist for twenty-six years, lives in Mumbai with her family. A short story by her featured in the humour anthology, *Jest Like That*, published in 2018.

IT'S ALSO ABOUT
MYNAH

RUCHA CHITRODIA

AMARYLLIS

AMARYLLIS

An imprint of Manjul Publishing House Pvt. Ltd.
• C-16, Sector 3, Noida, Uttar Pradesh 201301, India
Website: www.manjulindia.com
Registered Office:
• 10, Nishat Colony, Bhopal 462 003 – India

Copyright © Rucha Chitrodia 2021

Rucha Chitrodia asserts the moral right to be
identified as the author of this work

ISBN 978-93-90085-69-9

Cover design: Devi Kesari

Prologue

UMBRELLAS BLOOMED AS MYNAH BEGAN TO CLIMB THE incline that led to her gated apartment complex but she didn't reach for hers in the black tote. Bring it on, she muttered under her breath, and sprinted towards her apartment wing, past a blur of gulmohars, coconut palms, frangipanis and a gigantic banyan tree, its wide trunk wound in white thread by married women for their husbands' health and longevity.

She lurched breathless into the waiting elevator in C Wing of the complex in Lalbaug, a central district in Mumbai, Bombay or Bambai, as the island city is called by its people and visitors, and visitors who go on to become its people.

Liftman Raja Jadhav—a person who could not further shrink nor age his underfed body—welcomed her in with a 'good evening'. The pleasantry reached his eyes because Mynah's T-shirt was clinging to her.

The other person who had entered the elevator along with her looked intently at the screen ahead that flashed numbers of storeys crested in an ascending order, as if mesmerized by their progress. His studied indifference made

Mynah, panting against the steel-bodied elevator wall, smile faintly in gratitude.

The elevator dinged to a stop on the fourth floor and she got out, thanking the liftman out of habit and bidding a breezy 'bye' to the other man who wished her back with a startled smile.

At least my umbrella is dry, thought Mynah as she looked for a towel in her room.

She woke the next morning to heaviness and chill. The floor of her room in Aruna's flat where she lived as a paying guest felt cold as she walked barefoot to the long mirror on the wardrobe and looked into her swollen eyes. She walked back to her bed and let herself fall into it with a thud.

Aruna's muffled voice rose from the drawing room.

'Mynah, are you okay?'

'I'm running a temperature, aunty. Must be at least a hundred and four. No, a hundred and five. Remember, I got totally drenched yesterday? I am dying now.'

'Don't die right away. Let me get you some ginger tea first.'

'That,' said Mynah, 'would be awesome.'

As Aruna tiptoed in, Mynah jumped up to give her a hug, unmindful of passing on germs, and fell into the bed back again, this time with Aruna, both giggling.

Rohit, the fourteenth-floor resident of the fourteen-storey Jamuna Heights, was twitchy with anticipation as he entered the elevator the next morning. He willed it to stop on the fourth floor.

It didn't.

.

Chapter 1

'SO WHAT'S THE PROBLEM, MA?'

Dr Murali Radhakrishnan was seated in a window-less cabin in the farthest corner of his packed clinic in the city's southern Fort locality, named after a fortified structure built during the reign of the East India Company.

Mynah and her guardians—Aruna and part-time help Susheela—were in no mood to admire the worn-out colonial buildings. They had gotten off the taxi an hour ago and killed time in the doctor's waiting room.

Right in the middle of the large waiting room, bordered by benches for patients, hung a majestic swing with ornate silver prongs fastened on to a wooden slab on its two sides. The significance of the swing was not obvious to visitors such as Aruna who had never met Dr Radhakrishnan before but had read his opinion on mental health issues in newspapers and had therefore sought him out for Mynah. Dr Radhakrishnan told his juniors the swing, which moved like a pendulum under a large fan, was intended to lull his patients into a more receptive frame of mind.

✤

The doctor looked at the young woman with southern curls, milk chocolate skin and abnormally large and unusual yellow eyes. Her nose curved delicately towards her full brown lips.

'He just left me like that and does not take my calls,' Dr Radhakrishnan heard Mynah tell him.

'Then stop calling him,' replied the doctor simply.

'We are so close that I never have to think before picking up the phone. I just call. But why doesn't he pick up? He must have seen my thousand missed calls. What has changed? My father did not like him but what does that have to do with us?' she presented her perplexity without expression. This moved the doctor who had never managed to not get moved by young women.

Stage one, he thought.

Mynah turned her golden eyes to the floor and kept playing with her fingers, clenching and unclenching them to an inaudible rhythm.

She spoke after a period of silence since Dr Radhakrishnan had responded to her laments with his. He wanted to hear her out.

'All my dad told him was that we had an estate and that I would inherit it. I don't even know how the topic came up and that too during their first meeting. Rohit looked very upset.'

'Perhaps your boyfriend asked about it.'

'No. I had already told him a long time back.'

'Is your dad generally rude?'

'Never.'

'Do you think he brought up the topic to gauge what your boyfriend feels for you?'

'Rohit loves me. I've known it from the first time I saw him. He once kissed my feet. Both. He gets me so many gifts. He's very well-placed in his job as a landscape architect. Why would he be keen on my dad's estate in a remote, god-forsaken place? What would he do with it? He's been in Mumbai all his life.'

'Sell it?'

'Who will buy? There is no market for farm estates now, even cash crop. Why would he want dud land?'

'So you believe Rohit felt insulted.'

'But he can tell me so if he did,' Mynah's voice was a low wail. 'I want to hear his voice. Why shut me out like this? Overnight. Everything changed in that one meeting. Everything. It's all turned topsy-turvy.'

The doctor wanted to smile as he had not heard the usage in a long time. It took him back to his school when a teacher, Sujata ma'am, had made him repeat it ten times as he had mouthed 'tospy-turvy'. He was eight then, a plump boy his mother considered too thin and insisted on feeding five meals a day. He hated food for years because of it but missed the attention now that he had come to depend on a walking stick.

Reluctantly, he returned to Mynah, her little world and her regular problem. 'Okay, ma, give me his number. I'll call him.'

'You will? Do psychiatrists call people? Is it allowed? He does not even know that I have been taken to one. Aruna aunty recommended you and so we are here. Just for consultation. Otherwise I would have been sleeping in my room. I have not been able to step out since that day. That was three days ago. Three whole days. I began to shiver when I tried to get dressed yesterday and aunty had to put me under a hot shower to warm me up. Then I threw up and a little something came out of my nose as well. I feel like sleeping all the time and hope when I wake up things are back to normal. But when I wake up, I remember they are not. It all comes back in a rush and I feel like sleeping again to forget that he does not want to speak to me anymore. Does it not pain him that he has not spoken to me for three days? Is three an unlucky number? Maybe he'll pick up the phone tomorrow.'

'What are you feeling right now?'

'I don't feel anything, to be honest. I just want to hold him and not feel sleepy. I know I'll be alright then. But what if he does not want to speak to me ever?'

'You can sleep as much as you want, ma. Don't expect

answers just yet. Forget about it all for a day.'

'How can I forget anything for a day? Can I stop my mind from thinking about him when I cannot think of anything else?'

'I ask only for a day. I'll give you a small tablet that will make you forget things for a while. Take it before you sleep.'

'But why should I forget?'

Dr Radhakrishnan was also a hypnotist. He met Mynah's eyes and made contact with her through the haze. She nodded and went out for a psychometric test for which she was made to look at triangles and squares and blots of colourful ink, asked to describe them and then to write down stuff about herself, her thoughts, her dreams, her nightmares, her past, her expectations. No one had ever wanted to know her this well. If she were whole, she would have laughed at this inordinately high amount of interest in her.

Chapter 2

Rohit was beautiful. His eyes were a dark brown, lips pink and thin and dipping in all the right places, nose straight and adequate, and skin translucent. His cheeks shone like rubies in Mumbai's all-weather humidity. Robust women fell for his dainty appeal at sight. The more feminine capitulated soon upon finding a man who spoke their language and who was willing to share his torturous life story with them rather than act collected and male. He spoke easily of his father's struggles as a professor who plodded till he saved enough to open his own coaching school. He expounded the family's move to a flat in leafy Kalina, the eastern counterpart of the western suburb of Santacruz, closer to the city centre than their former one in what he called mofussil Dahisar up north. The move was a happy result of success, after flyers of Professor Trivedi's Coaching Class in Borivali, also up north, began to be distributed along with morning newspapers, and students who aimed to graduate with jaw-dropping scores lined up at the 800-square-foot commercial space he had rented to teach. Rohit often underscored his mother's sacrifice in bringing them up with limited cash and without a maid or a husband available to help her. Some women would pat his hand at that and feel tenderness well up inside them.

'I had to chip in with housework and sweep and swab the floor whenever she was unwell, even during exams. Mohit, my brother, was the baby of the house, so we never asked him to do anything. But it's no big deal.'

He would dole out the line with a self-effacing smile. A rope trick that made him climb right up women's estimation of him.

༄

Mynah reached home after work to a laid table.

Aruna insisted she finish three chapatis with dal, a salad and a leafy vegetable first. After the feeding came the slaughter.

'A cute man was here looking for a young girl who had dropped a book in the elevator while getting off on the fourth floor. He said he was guilty of keeping it with him for so long. Mynah, you have an admirer.'

'What book is it?' asked Mynah, looking distractedly for the television remote.

Her reaction was typical. Aruna laughed and got up to get it.

'It is called, let me see, *Resurrection at the Workplace*.'

Mynah grimaced and gestured with her hands to imply why would she even hold such a book.

'But he seems like a well-read fellow. This book is written by that famous psychiatrist, Dr Wu.'

'Shrinks find time to write books? That's news to me, dude. I should write a book on what happened to his patients.'

Aruna grinned and ran a hand through Mynah's curls.

'Don't you want to know anything about him?' she asked tenderly.

'Yes. I will have to give it back to him. Where does he live?' asked Mynah, more than a little flattered.

Rohit had wanted Mynah since his encounter with her breezy 'bye'. He began to go up and down the two passenger elevators in their wing a couple of times a day and sat out free hours on a couch in the entrance lobby of the apartment wing pretending to read on his phone in the hope of bumping into the wet girl. On Day Six he got off on the fourth floor with the book and knocked on the door the girl had approached that evening.

A woman opened it.

He felt a surge and forgot reason. Her mouth, bosom, curvaceous frame, indifferently rolled up hair, arms akimbo, head a little tilted and knowing light eyes obliterated all else till she spoke.

'Yes?' asked Aruna, eyebrows raised, in a flat, matter-of-fact tone.

Clearing his throat, he said, 'I was looking for a girl who had dropped this book in the elevator about a week ago. I am guilty of keeping it with me for so long. I had seen her get in here. Is she around?'

Aruna looked at the boy and knew he was in the market and had put her in the shopping trolley as well.

'She's not home but I'll ask her about it when she returns,' she said, trying to sound stern and succeeding.

'What's her name, please? Just in case,' he asked, his throat dry.

'Mynah. Where do you stay?'

'I'm on the fourteenth floor. Flat 1403. Mynah. That's a lovely name. I'm Rohit.'

He held out his hand. Aruna did not offer hers.

'I'll tell her,' she said, still unsmiling.

'Thank you, ma'am. And what's your name, please, if I may ask?'

He conjured up a silky smile.

'Aruna aunty,' she replied and pursed her lips.

Rohit stiffened and left after bowing in an Oriental fashion, unconsciously copied from Hong Kong wuxia movies. Aruna had no desire to play the field and definitely not with Mynah's suitor in this life or the next.

Before Subodh, her former husband, she had two

boyfriends in college, whose names she had a tough time recollecting. She had been consumed by Subodh for years and now wondered whether even he was real and existed outside her head.

Chapter 3

SUBODH HAD GIFTED THE LALBAUG FLAT TO ARUNA AS an apology for leaving her, a home they had shared for several rancour-less years. Till the formal parting, Aruna had operated like a rich man's poodle that must be sheared and beautified in pet salons and brought back home to a master to perform lovable feats. Dog's fate for forging an alliance with Man millennia ago, relinquishing pride for loyalty and a shot at survival—which must not be confused with living.

When he had begun divorce proceedings, Aruna had found herself in a dog pound, thrashing about for an escape to what was safe, what was known, to sorted days and weekends.

But long before formalization of the parting, for Aruna, the one big perk of being a couple had gotten entangled in cobwebs—the tactile. The hugs and the cuddles had shrunk. The shrinkage could be passed off as the usual trajectory of man-woman kinship, the end result of prolonged familiarity that envelops and cushions couples over years of being with one another, preparing them to move beyond the physical, for the body itself grows out of its own self and must get used to its final moving away. Aruna's case was not to be confused with this common pattern though.

It was her house help Susheela who had come up with the idea of seeking a paying guest to fill Aruna's days. A dog, a cat or even a mute turtle would have meant nurturing. Susheela thought her madam was not up to it. She suggested an adult human for company.

Aruna had no avenue of entertainment outside of Subodh and his circle. She had never cultivated her own friends or interacted with the women who sat near the banyan, morning and evening, on the steps that led to a white marble temple of Lord Krishna in a mini forest in the building complex. Seated on the steps, the women would catch up on their day that must follow other days in a straight file. They would be out in full force most days, the reins of their kitchens left in the able hands of cooks. Grown children would be with their tuition teachers or on their phones or playing in the lawn nearby, and their husbands at that point would be another point of discussion, a mere idea.

Aruna had only moved in a cosmopolitan stratosphere with her husband. Subodh's friends were senior corporate executives. They were married to their corporate wives, most of whom did not make friends with other corporate wives. They networked. They did not invite people home. They hosted them. Aruna had quickly adopted the culture as was expected of her. Wives of Subodh's friends had become hers till Subodh had walked away with the friendships.

If Aruna had children she would have had things to share with some of the women who sat near the banyan. She joined them one evening, made small talk, but had little to contribute to what was being said and could make little sense of anything. A paying guest made sense.

But when the first paying guest arrived with her bags, Aruna felt violated on seeing a strange woman unpack things in what had been her spare bedroom.

Aruna had an aversion to strange women.

She cleaned the room after the woman left for work and then waited for her return in the evening. The cleaning stopped within days and she began to live vicariously through her. The woman could do as she pleased, bring guests home and share her room for a few days. Six months later, she quit her job as a producer with an entertainment television channel and the city too.

Had Gopala, Mynah's father, stooped by an inherited farm estate and self-imposed rectitude, known of the permissive bent of the flat-owner, he would have scrolled down the lease listings he was browsing for his only child in a strange city. He was afraid of women of will.

Mynah had moved to Mumbai from Bengaluru or Bangalore, another city with multiple names, to join Ad Grande as copywriter thirteen months back. It was her first job five months after a post-convocation party with other students of her journalism institute at JP Nagar, not too far from her home in Jayanagar, its bungalows hidden in a lush avenue where genteel people led genteel lives. It was walking distance from a large, wild botanical zone named Lalbagh where humans did not live. They visited. It was nothing like the eponymous, though differently spelled, crowded locality of Lalbaug in Mumbai where Mynah was wiping her hair in her room and fantasizing about a hot bath to wash off rainwater.

Back home in Bangalore, on another rainy day, Mynah and her classmates had trooped into a pub opposite their institute for the graduation party. Mynah had sipped on Peach Sundowner, a mocktail her father approved of. She had been back home by seven, right after sundown, in a car that had waited outside the pub till her drink was drunk.

Gopala had tagged along with Mynah to Mumbai for her job interview and, when his daughter thought she stood a chance of bagging the job, tried to frighten her into staying back with him in Bangalore. She had reasoned that it was a tight job market and she had not got placed even in a local newspaper or a web portal in her home city.

'Advertising is not too different from journalism, Daddy. It involves writing too,' she had argued determinedly.

Gopala had gazed on, his heart full, at twenty-one-year-old Mynah's still rounded cheeks, the open eyes that had seen little more than dreams, dreams that made her present her case with the animation of a fledgling.

My little Baby, he thought.

Gopala had promptly begun to scour the internet for flats in areas considered safe in Mumbai, which he thought of simplistically as a city of bomb blasts. Mynah had laughed and patted her father's hand while turning down his plans to send along the cook and the driver, both known to her since she was a Baby—her pet name too. She wanted to live alone.

'It's high time, Daddy. Shloka has been living in Delhi all by herself, and that is the most dangerous city in the entire whole world. She takes the metro every single day and returns late at night after ten o'clock. No one has kidnapped her and no one has blasted the metro, for God's sake.'

He had laughed in reflex, momentarily home, for she had hugged him and given him a peck. Just as quickly, he had pulled himself back to the present that loomed despite the sunniness of his child.

Mynah had taken his hand and spoken with as much

bravado as she could muster: 'Daddy. Trust me. I'll always take Uber or Ola and you'll get my travel status once it starts and after it drops me.'

She had then held out her hand in a mock-oath and declared: 'I hereby solemnly pledge to never use public transport. I shall never set foot inside a shared taxi. I shall never help strangers who pretend to be lost in the city or ask for alms, even if they shed big, big, fat, fat tears. I shall not go for movies alone, even for morning or afternoon shows. Promise, promise, promise...'

To keep himself from overthinking and to come to terms with the inevitable, Gopala read up articles on terror attacks to tick off, one by one, what he thought of as bomb-blast localities of Mumbai—Colaba, Fort, Crawford Market, Zaveri Bazaar, Opera House, Worli, Dadar, Matunga, Mahim, Bandra, Khar Road, Santacruz, Vile Parle, Jogeshwari, Borivli, Ghatkopar and Mulund—where random lives were annihilated in separate batches between 1993 and 2011. The first series of coordinated explosions was aimed at avenging the communal riots of 1992, in the aftermath of the demolition of a mosque in the northern state of Uttar Pradesh more than a thousand kilometres from Mumbai, a city surrounded on all its sides by the Arabian Sea off the beauteous coast of the western state of Maharashtra.

Thereon, after the riots, even the slight Gopala, who spent his days bent at the waist tending to colourful anthuriums under a canopy of mother of cocoa and beech trees in the compound of his single-storey bungalow in Bangalore in the southern Karnataka state, even farther from Ayodhya than Maharashtra's capital of Mumbai, sometimes thought of his friends' religious identities.

The ghosts of blast victims, former people, clung to Gopala after he stopped browsing his phone while slouched on a chair in his verandah. There were so many of them and Mynah was his only child.

Gopala zeroed in on the room in a two-bedroom flat in the fetching Jamuna Heights in the locality of Lalbaug, where fortunately no blast had taken place. He called the number and was relieved to hear a 'well-educated, ladylike voice of a capable-sounding woman'. The flat, the post on leasequickly.com had read, was owned by a single, middle-aged woman who wanted to give out her spare bedroom to another single woman. Gopala had felt reassured since she had not specified 'young woman' as a criterion; that would have raised his parental antennae.

The woman had demanded thirty thousand rupees a month and a steep deposit of two lakh rupees upfront. She knew her market.

Few leased rooms or homes to singletons in Mumbai, for they could be murderers, terrorists, fraudsters or seducers. A decade or so ago, a man caught in a rivalrous love triangle had been hacked in a flat in Malad, a north-western suburb populated by an incongruous mix of small-time diamond merchants, artificial jewellery traders, and back offices of certain corporate and media houses due to the affordability factor of the real estate. For the same reason, Malad was also home to an expanding community of middling migrant television actors and struggling film artistes. Two of the personae dramatis in the murder had been of the struggler variety. The dazed owner of the bloodied flat where the man had been killed was left blinking at police and media scrutiny with a home loan that could not be offset by rental income. It was only years after the crime that the owner managed to sell the flat, following collective public amnesia that invariably trails celebrity.

࿓

Gopala's ghosts had lived inside of him, straining against a corroded leash that snapped and set them free at the tug of Mynah's leaving.

He quickly agreed to the flat-owner's asking price, wanting the safest weather-proof nest for Mynah, his daughter who was named after that small bird with a brown body, its plumage interspersed with white flecks and its black eyes bordered with fine chrome-yellow feathers.

He had wiped his sweaty neck on finding the flat a few

kilometres from his child's imminent workplace in the flashy central business district of Parel, also home to the moneyed and those coming to terms with the moneyed moving into their working-class area.

Here he deposited, with a mad beating heart, his precious little girl bird.

Chapter 4

Mynah was seated opposite three senior executives of Ad Grande. They were going through the portfolio of articles she had written at the journalism institute. She smiled at Ashok, the art director, when he met her eyes.

'So, Mynah, you have written a report on intelligent building management systems. An interesting and, if I may say so, odd choice of subject for a journalism student. It's rather niche. More a B2B construction industry kind of an article. Why did you choose this topic?' he asked.

'Sir...' Mynah started.

'Call me Ash,' he said.

'Ash sir, I wrote it because my module coordinator asked me to,' she replied.

'You did not choose it?' he asked kindly.

'No, sir.'

'Well, you seem to have done a lot of legwork for it.'

Mynah beamed and the words tumbled out: 'Yes, sir. I visited four premium housing societies and two commercial complexes and spoke to two property management consultancies and one environmentalist.'

Ash exchanged a quiet smile with Pradyuman 'Pad', the executive creative director. Rakesh 'Rake', the creative associate, scowled at the cute, nauseating scene which he recounted to the amusement of his colleagues after Mynah left.

'I got two hundred and nineteen Facebook likes for the piece,' Mynah was saying enthusiastically.

Pad, grey at the temples and father to a teenager, wanted to pat her shoulder. Rake thought it was time to intervene.

'Can you show me?' he asked brusquely, to spot a lie if it were being told.

'Yes, yes, sir.'

Rake did not ask her to call him Rake. As he scrolled down her mobile phone, he read her status updates and photo captions.

'Rads r u in Blr or out? If aren't in, I'm out.'

'A rainbow on the Masinagudi sky looks like a drop of petrol on a puddle. Same effect :)'

'Wind against my face, woohoo! I'm flying to Warsaw on a plane to launch a war. Wait a minute! I don't even know what Warsaw is. Is it a place, a bird or an aeroplane? Read the name somewhere. Wait a minute! The aircraft has its sunglasses on. My hair's flying. hahahahaa LOL'

'You wrote this?' Rake barked.

'Yes, sir. But it was just for fun, among friends,' she said.

'Why do you wish to join advertising?' Rake asked, businesslike.

'My friend saw the ad on LinkedIn and told me to apply as I wasn't getting any other job in any case.'

Mynah got an offer letter three weeks later. Copywriter, a six-month probation and twenty-five thousand rupees in monthly salary.

Chapter 5

M YNAH'S ABSENCE FROM GOPALA'S HOUSEHOLD OF TWO saw him while away the hours rearranging furniture and dusting them twice a day, in the morning and at dusk. In between he watched the news on television, chatted up the cook, the maid and the driver since he did not feel like stepping out and meeting his many friends. Gopala had also taken to forgetting to use his home diabetes counter and to call up the manager of his farm estate at day end, and had to be reminded to wire the money to pay rubber tappers and labourers on Fridays. In a first, he missed giving the chartered accountant his annual plantation income tax papers. This omission did not ruffle him when sternly reminded of it by the old accountant, as Gopala had now begun to live with Mynah in a duplicate world. The reality outside his head was an irritant to be tolerated and gotten out of the way.

On weekdays, Gopala would walk out with Mynah from the Lalbaug flat when she would text the mutually pre-decided 'LW' code for 'Left for Work'. He would travel with her in the cab and see the narrow lane merge with a large arterial road and take a left to hit a flyover to cross over to the western side of Parel where her office was situated. Had she reached office? She was supposed to text him 'RD' for 'Reached, Daddy'. On leaving office, 'LO' for 'Left Office'. On reaching the flat in the evening, 'RF'. If she were ever in danger, she was to shoot off a 'D'. Gopala had unsteadily given those instructions to Mynah while leaving her behind in Mumbai a day before she was to join work. He had left after placing his faith in Aruna who discomfited him with her direct stare and tight smile, but her eyes were not unkind.

Gopala had not remarried since the vanishing of Mynah's mother with her lover with whom she had re-stitched a relationship torn by the pragmatism of her parents. Gracy's marriage to Gopala had sated their need for societal validation. He was the only son of a moneyed plantation owner who was to inherit a hundred and ten acres of a rubber estate interspersed with patches of teak trees and black pepper and clove shrubs near Nilambur town in the northern region of the southern-most state of Kerala. The large chunk of land that Gopala went on to own was dunked in chlorophyll that completely hid the red soil underneath.

Gracy had bumped into her lover, the money-challenged Hemanth who worked as a telephone operator in a starred hotel, at a grocery store in Indiranagar, not too far from her Jayanagar home. An eight-month pregnant Gracy and Hemanth had reaffirmed their love in his rented flat; sideways, to avoid the baby bump.

Gracy fed Mynah for three months after her birth, which the new mother thought was the adequate amount of breast milk required for an infant. She left after putting Mynah to sleep and dialling Gopala, asking him to rush home for an emergency. He had found an unattended Mynah in her cot with a note responsibly sticking out of her little pillow that announced Gracy's exit from her arranged marriage and motherhood. He heard from a ubiquitous well-wisher years later that she had left her bachelor boyfriend for his married brother who then put her up in a flat somewhere in Bangalore. The well-wisher had regretted that he did not have her address, though Gopala had not asked for it. She did not have any more children with either brother.

Gopala dreamt of her often, as the jilted must do, leading a parallel life in his dreams that leaves behind a residue of emptiness on waking.

Aruna had heard Gopala's worry for his child when he had called her first. She would know.

She had met Subodh in college during her most sought-after phase of youth, for her blue-violet eyes, jet black straight hair, and grace that comes with sexual confidence, something that the beautiful take in their stride as a given. Subodh radiated intelligence and ambition. His spectacles reflected even more light off his skin. The duo attracted envy.

He studied management after college and Aruna worked as an accountant with a real estate firm. She found the job boring but sat it out till Subodh picked her up in the evenings. He would drop her outside her hostel at night before the ten o'clock curfew.

He soon got placed in a leading bank as a junior executive, earned the better appraisals year on year and rose to become a senior vice-president, and never felt the need to switch jobs, a rarity among his peers.

A year into his job, he married Aruna who left hers and began to spend her days first doing up their home and then redecorating it at regular intervals while continuing to wait for him in the evenings.

The couple did not graduate to parenthood, the expected next step for many, as Subodh was short on sperm. The deficiency was a result of, the doctor had consoled him after a series of tests some years into their marriage, his high-pressure job and work hours. Subodh was advised a six-month sabbatical.

'Go on an extended vacation with your beautiful wife. Give her some of your precious time and precious sperm,' the doctor had said gently. Fertility experts are advised to use humour as their job involves putting depressed patients at ease and helping them deal with their innermost deficiencies wrapped inside their briefs and panties.

Subodh had not laughed at the doctor's joke. He had stormed out of the clinic and waited in the car for Aruna who had run after him, flushed with embarrassment. The silent journey had taken the two to their previous flat in Prabhadevi, another central locality, but this one lining the sea. Subodh had walked into the windy bedroom heavily and bolted the door.

He did not ever go on a vacation with Aruna. He chose to return home late and meet friends over weekends with her to rule out alone time. He bought a new flat, the one at Lalbaug, months after the visit to the doctor's clinic, in an area where no one knew him or would know him.

Unknown to Aruna, Subodh had always flirted with women at work and taken lovers. Nine months after the episode at the doctor's, he brought one to his new home.

Aruna had opened the door and smiled, befuddled at the appearance of the guest. Subodh was not in the habit of coming back with anyone. But he had walked the strange woman in that evening by hand, a fact that seared Aruna. She had asked the woman, pretty in a flowy Friday dress, whether she would like some tea, coffee or a drink, hot or cool. The woman had shrugged a no, thank you, and Subodh and she had gone on to sit on the couch. Aruna had looked for ways to entertain the appearance of the arctic newness. She entered the kitchen, opened drawers and shut them and then sat on a stool for a while. When she came out, Subodh and the woman had fused into a solitary being. He had smiled at Aruna on seeing her look on uncomprehendingly and mechanically pour out a glass of red wine to go with the paneer tikkis she had prepared as a starter for dinner.

After a lifetime that flashed in and out of her head, she had turned and wobbled into the washroom, glass in hand, to lean against the sink to vomit, and then mourned on the cold uncut granite floor that the interior decorator had promised was slippage-proof. Drained, she had come out and found him watching the television, its flickering images reflecting off his glasses and shielding his eyes. He was alone. She had waited for the sound of the door latch to open and shut to pull herself up and leave the security of the washroom. He had looked up and smiled at her easily and returned his eyes to the screen.

Aruna could not bring herself to scream out her objection to what had transpired inside her home. A long habit of congeniality could not be broken. Besides, she was aware of the lines around her eyes, her sagging cheeks, her large dimpled breasts that needed a good bra, her patchy skin and tiny bumps of cherry angioma on her body, and that she had not held a job for years. Her parents, Rajesh and

Suman, were dead and had left her and her brother Suyash, a doctor, a tiny flat back home in Kothrud in Pune city, about a hundred and fifty kilometres from Mumbai. The Pune flat would fetch her forty lakh rupees at best, which would have to be divided equally with her brother who lived in the United States and who had consciously limited his ties with the family back home. He had never invited his parents over to his five-bedroom house with a basement, a lawn, a backyard and a three-car parking space in Houston. He did not want his peers to know his ordinary-looking parents had been school teachers who had forgone an option for pension at retirement in favour of a lump sum provident fund—a few lakh rupees each. His parents could not afford a maid or presentable clothes with the interest earned on that kind of money, a fact that embarrassed Suyash who was easily embarrassed. He sent twenty thousand rupees to them every month for a few years after their retirement—till the twins with his Spanish wife came along. The doctor who earned upwards of two hundred and fifty thousand dollars a year plugged the largesse to his parents, citing financial constraints. The phone call broke them. Rajesh died within two years of the call and Suman a year after him. Suyash came down for both funerals and wept with a genuine feeling of release.

His wife and children did not accompany him both times. The only person Suyash met effusively at both the funerals was Subodh, his social equal. Aruna knew that the collapse of her marriage would mean the Diwali, Christmas and New Year greeting cards from her oncologist brother, who had emigrated from India eighteen years ago, would stop.

Aruna sat next to Subodh that evening and sobbed noiselessly. He reached out to caress her hair for a while and slept in her arms.

Over long years, Subodh brought home three more women, all underlings at work. Each episode lasted a few months but for one. The woman had looked at Aruna with open sympathy and insisted on leaving. Once Subodh had asked Aruna to join a lover. But she had walked past, by now immune to his capacity to inflict pain and the woman had laughed.

He came home one evening with pleading eyes and Aruna nodded a yes. Subodh offered to buy his way out of her life while insisting he felt a lot of affection for her.

Aruna paid attention after years and asked, 'How much?'

Choking back tears, he said, 'Two crores in your account and this flat and everything that's in it.'

'Fine,' said Aruna and went to the kitchen to turn on the microwave.

Chapter 6

ARUNA TOOK TO MYNAH INSTANTLY. THE INVOLUNTARILY childless do not lose time in getting attached to children and the child-like. Besides, Mynah, younger than most girls her age because of her upbringing, had inherited Gracy's charm. She lunged at Aruna's heart with her impromptu and thoughtful offers.

'Auntyji, surprise! I've got you an XL top in black to make you look super-duper thin. Not that you're fat, bro. You look M to me. Come on, try it on.'

'Aruna aunty darling, GoT's on. You watch, I'll get you a cheese sandwich. The low-fat one. Don't worry, I'll catch the episode later.'

'You want to give me company for the blues gig? I know all your old songs. I've got a pass for you. Just the two of us.'

Mynah was by herself most evenings and weekends in an unknown city and Aruna's social circle had shrunk to the circumference of a finger ring after the divorce. That alone time together worked as glue. Aruna would do up Mynah's hair and squeeze her shoulders when done. She would then get up to heat a traditional lunch of rice and bland dal or a fragrant dish of steamed rice, lentils, vegetables and invigorating spices, which she would pack for her tiffin. On certain weekends, she would roll out a soft, doughy wheat bread and stuff it with a filling of cottage cheese, potatoes and peas.

Aruna's culinary prowess had been seriously honed by her mother with the sole aim of pleasing the husband, whoever he was, and all those who mattered to him, whoever they were. Now, her marinating skills thrilled her paying guest who had not known a mother, though to be fair, she had known an indulgent grandmother. Mynah looked forward to seeing aunty in the evenings and sharing her day with her, and Aruna to listening on.

༈

Inside flat number 401 Subodh was smiling fondly at Aruna as she offered him water. He was visiting after close to three years. His first after his leaving.

'How did he go?' asked Aruna politely about his brother Vinod.

'Pressure dropped and he slipped into a coma,' said Subodh as he took in the new divan, side sofas and the dining table. The flat looked unfamiliar.

Aruna began to ask, 'His heart was...'

'Still thirty per cent functional,' he completed her sentence.

'How is Linzy?' asked Aruna, knowing well what the answer would be.

'She looks positively overjoyed. Not making any attempt to hide her glee.'

They laughed.

'I'll go visit,' Aruna lied. She had no reason to.

'Don't forget to carry some champagne. She's taken to popping the cork at daybreak. Teju is in Minnesota. He's got an internship there with a company, I forget the name. Calls her sometimes. Not often enough,' said Subodh, trying to look dejected on Linzy's behalf.

'At least he calls,' said Aruna in reflex.

Subodh walked up and took her in his arms.

'I failed you,' he said.

Aruna shrugged but did not pull away.

'You didn't, Subodh. I failed myself. I was too beautiful to think of doing anything with my life other than being with you,' she said truthfully.

'You are still beautiful,' said Subodh, choosing to ignore her statement.

Aruna freed herself from the bear hug at that and looked into his eyes.

'What will you have?' she asked.

'Daniels,' he answered expectedly.

You *are still*, not you *are*, she thought.

Aruna relived the hour till she slept off. It was late in the afternoon. She had expected him to have aged but his stomach was still flat, his muscular arms were dumbbell-enhanced and he had shaded his hair a becoming brown. He was wearing a slim-fit shirt and distressed jeans. Aruna wondered whether his new look was an upgrade or symptomatic of insecurity. A Movember that poked her face when he hugged her had felt foreign like the rest of him. He had always been a yuppie in his choice of places to visit but had not followed trends in dressing or grooming. Must be Harsha, she thought.

Aruna did not ask about the woman for whom he had transferred the flat to her name. She had seen them sing John Lennon's *Imagine* at a party the former couple had thrown at home. Harsha and Subodh had not looked at each other at all that evening. Aruna had assumed she would be brought home again. She wasn't. He had walked out.

Harsha was self-assured in her old-money swag. She had passed out of a girls' boarding school in the port city of Visakhapatnam which had adopted a faux ancient system of education. Here students lived in huts and carried out tasks for teachers like sweeping the floor of their rooms and laying out their meals. After the students kept the brooms aside, ayahs would take over. They would also cook the food the students were meant to gingerly hold, carry and offer their teachers. Students suffered this kind of drudgery in their air-conditioned huts. On the upside, they were taken on many field trips and not expected to memorise chapters like parakeets, as students enrolled in the blinkered, mainstream education system ought to. The students at this school were expected to internalise whatever they studied. That was all. What the girls loved the most was being prodded to give vent to expression in any manner, form and degree they wished, without sticking to the median. Conservative parents feared sending their wards to the school, worried their girls would become too independent and averse to a conformist life. It was true that many of the students who passed out of the cool huts after learning to play the veena or the guitar, to move to the traditional Kuchipudi dance as well as the Colombian Zumba, to essay intense roles in plays by Kalidasa as well as the Bard, and to proudly plant saplings were single.

The school was started by a wealthy idealist in the 1950s. It initially offered subsidised education to girls but the founder sank into debt as teachers had to be paid well to match the demands of the customised, high-maintenance curriculum. He had to charge fees. There was no other go. A few months into the changed regime, students began to complain of heat and dust as their parents now paid full fees and thought it their right to demand their paisa's worth. The school then began to accept generous donations in return for providing comfort to the children. The founder's reservations, expressed in a voice thinned by age, were drowned out by the new, savvy and vociferous management.

Every break, Harsha would grudgingly go back home to her mother Malini and stepfather Madhav, so in love was she with her alma mater and so out of it with her own people. Her distaste for vacations had another dimension to it. She was ugly. She would walk into the two annual parties her mother hosted during her long summer break and short winter break, and feel punched in her viscera by pity each time. Malini was beautiful and Harsha a living memory of her dead father.

Her flat chest caved in as she struggled to hide her five feet nine inches, tall for Indian girls. Her skin was an orchard of acne at puberty which she plucked at unselfconsciously. At fifteen, she had screamed at Malini and asked why she had chosen the ugliest man for a spouse who had just lasted long enough to father her. Even Madhav, whom she insisted on calling Madhu like her mother, was better by comparison.

Her philanthropist mother had raised a hand to slap her and then remembered to be charitable and quietly left the room. Harsha had broken a china figurine on seeing her mother walk away without responding or consoling her. A child's impotent revenge.

Harsha came into her own during her early youth when she grew her wavy hair long and artfully allowed it to graze her face and neck to hide fresh acne and scars of past ones. She could do little about the ones on her forehead but with effort learnt to keep her chin up. She wore clingy outfits that drew eyes away from her face and towards her flat chest but swore against wearing a padded bra after an aunt had hugged her and smirkingly mentioned her stone-like breasts, unmindful of the effect of the statement on a teenager flogged by rejection.

Harsha would sit provocatively in her little dresses and think up ways to draw attention, which she finally got when she went to New York University to major in English literature at twenty. In the dry and windy climate of the US, so unlike sultry Mumbai and Visakhapatnam of India, her acne subsided and then miraculously disappeared. She asked out an expat student from Chile and he agreed. More followed. She returned home a year later with a belief in her acquired attractiveness and with two missions.

She lay sprawled on the hand-woven ikat rug, resting her feet on the olive green leather ottoman with a wooden trim and brass rivets. She was in the sunken sitting area of the living room of her mother's four-bedroom flat in Kemps Corner, a traditionally wealthy hub in the city's south which got the country's first-ever flyover some fifty years earlier, its construction demonstrating yet again the unquestionable correlation between infrastructure and the financial muscle to get it done.

Friends of the family would nod appreciatively at the understated interiors of the flat, its otherwise bare pastel walls displaying a single, astonishing painting. The floor on which Harsha was lolling was of a contrasting dark stained walnut hardwood. The sheer curtains with alternating drapes of indigo and ivory flew this way and that way to let in sea breeze from the french windows that opened out to a terrace, its left decorated with potted plants, right with a daybed and a lounging chair and the middle left vacant to stand and take in the open skies above and a park below.

Harsha was waiting for her bait. Madhav walked in and muttered something under his breath in his usual dismissive manner. Malini was away and Harsha had smoked up. He sniffed out the sweetness in the air.

'Have you done pot in my house?' he asked, trying to sound menacing.

Harsha met the threat in his voice with a cool, 'Madhu, this is my house as much as yours.'

'Listen. I'll tell your mother and then let's see what she has to say about it,' he tried to cow her down.

Harsha laughed and held his gaze.

'What will you tell her?'

Madhav could not look away. He was just a man.

The balding art collector, whose parents had owned an iron ore mine before filing for bankruptcy and who now survived on alms doled out by his wife, was not allowed near Harsha again.

Her second mission involved exacting his knowledge of the art world, his contacts and good offices. Years later, she even did a diploma in modern and contemporary Indian art and curatorial studies at Dr Bhau Daji Lad Museum in Byculla, eastwards from her home.

Her independent bent, a gift of her school, gave her skill an eccentric sharpness. She set up the Harsha Art Gallery in Colaba, a hipster district at the city's southern-most end, and curated works for industrial houses and homes of those who call in curators.

Subodh had been taken in by the unabashed look in her eyes when she had not let go of his hand which she had taken without a word spoken. They were at an event that he and Altaf, the chief executive officer of the bank where he worked, had been invited to.

'Hello. I want you,' she had said pointedly, eyes firmly locked with his, then a stranger.

'Is this how you greet people?' he had gotten out of his mouth, paralysed by the shock and thrill of the encounter.

'Only people I want.'

Harsha had told him to ditch the party and drop her home after ordering her driver to go ahead. She had rested her hand on his thigh, enjoying the build-up and his erratic driving till he had stopped the car outside her three-storey building and was grateful to have arrived without incident. Harsha, who lived with her mother and stepfather on the third floor, did not step out of the darkened vehicle for a while.

Subodh would not have got hooked if she had. She did not call or get in touch with him, so he did. She had given him her number, not asked for his. He called after a week.

He believed and then refused to disbelieve that with Harsha he would feel alive again and find an exciting anchor that he had in Aruna in their initial years. He wanted to feel wanted as a man who carried the promise of manliness. Aruna's wordless empathy at being told he would not be able to procreate without help had wounded him. Besides, he had turned fifty and was trying to come to terms with his diminishing attractiveness and other implications of mortality.

Harsha was thirty-nine and thought it was time she settled with a man who could critique Milan Kundera at parties. Subodh was self-made, not like Madhu who was born into money and had married into it. Her mother, Malini, had inherited two hundred acres of mango orchards and an old rent-generating commercial complex in the fertile town of Valsad in the coastal part of Gujarat, a state that borders Maharashtra to its north.

Madhav had once hit Harsha mercilessly when she had laughed and called him her mother's gigolo after overhearing him plead with Malini on the phone over an overdue credit card bill. He had stopped when she had threatened to tell her mother while trying to shield her body with her hands. As the broken man had left the room, he had heard the laughter resume.

Her man would be anything but a whiner and a loser.

Harsha had soon found that Subodh had no interest in literature or art, but by then she liked his otherwise quick mind and body. What she liked most about him was that he wanted to leave his clear-skinned voluptuous wife whom every man at the party he had hosted at his place wanted. Competition is an aphrodisiac.

Chapter 7

SUSHEELA GENTLY TAPPED ARUNA TILL SHE ROSE OUT OF her siesta.

'Madam, can you give me twenty thousand rupees? Suraj has fractured his arm again,' she mumbled between sobs.

'Oh, how?' asked Aruna out of politeness. She had no interest in Susheela's constant laments about her luckless son.

'Cricket. He's so weak. He eats just dal and lady's finger for lunch and dinner, day in and day out. I am fed up of cooking these two items for him. I feel like vomiting even while asking the vendor for lady's finger. But the one thing I do not compromise on is milk. I force him to drink almost a litre every day and yet he ends up breaking a bone. He'll be fired from his job one hundred and one per cent,' said Susheela.

'I have the money. What happened to your new friend, Kaveri? She had borrowed ten thousand from you, right? Has she returned it? You now have a valid reason to ask for it,' suggested Aruna.

Susheela slapped her forehead. 'She has disappeared. She did not even pay the brokerage to the agent for the room she had rented in the chawl right next to my place. I had introduced her to him and now I've lost face with that man. He'll never show me a room again as long as I live. He keeps calling me and asking me to pay up as if I have fled without paying him. She had borrowed from other maids in the complex as well.'

Aruna adopted a stern posture. 'I had told you not to give her even a rupee. Never be so trusting. If she could not afford to live in this part of town, she should not have tried to. You had barely known her a month.'

'Three months. But she cried so much. It was all acting, I know now,' said Susheela and remembered to resume sobbing. She could cry at the snap of a finger.

'At least it was a small amount,' said Aruna, pretending to sympathise while waiting for the exchange to end.

'Small for you, madam. I get that much from doing the dishes and cleaning two large flats in a month. All this hard labour for so many years has destroyed my back and knees. Look at my hands, they've become so rough. Like rocks. I've heard Kaveri's gone back to Nala Sopara where she came from. It is such a large place. Where will I find her?' wailed Susheela as Aruna got up to open her wallet to give her the money as advance payment that would be cut from her salary in monthly instalments.

❧

Some say Nala Sopara, sixty-five kilometres from Lalbaug and more than an hour's ride by train, came up near an ancient thriving port. The site of a Buddhist stupa, today the town has large shanty pockets that know little peace.

After a property boom in Mumbai in the early years of the new millennium, developers paid off slum-dwellers to take over their land to build apartments, effectively pushing them out of city limits. Nala Sopara in the neighbouring Palghar district, linked to Mumbai by the suburban railway network and a highway, began to fill with Mumbaikars who had previously pockmarked the city with their poverty. The neighbourhood maid likewise became a rarity as slums shrank and property prices of the leftover chawls and shanties matched what middle-income families paid to rent nano flats in middle-class buildings.

The maid moved to Nala Sopara to afford a roof at a rent of just a thousand rupees a month, an unheard of sum in Mumbai.

❧

She would wake up early before the sun heated up her shanty's corrugated sheet roof and line up at a public toilet with its half-eaten doors and broken windows without shutters. Some men would watch her go through her ablutions through the

windows and threaten to rape her. She would ignore them
and leave without meeting their eyes. She would then line
up with plastic buckets at a few undernourished taps illegally
provided by slumlords in connivance with amoral municipal
officials, and fight with other women to ensure she had
enough water for the day. Some of the fill would be used to
cook for the family. She would not have time to wolf down
the breakfast though, for it would be time to leave behind
her home and children for work in Mumbai. The children
would spend their days roaming around unmonitored.

The maid would wriggle her way into an airless, packed
local train where her hair would get pulled and sari crumpled.
She would push or be pushed out of the train by others
wanting to get off at the railway station closest to her
place of work. At the platform, she would sometimes haggle
with female vendors to buy a band for her hair naturally
dyed a dark blond by dirty bathing water and lack of care.
Sometimes she would pick up a necklace of tiny black beads
strung on a fake gold chain to be mandatorily worn around
her married neck. The vendor would invariably be a woman
who wore no jewellery.

The maid would walk out of the station and line up for
a public bus. Inside the crowded vehicle her shrivelled body
would get felt by faceless hands, an occupational hazard to
be tolerated till she reached her stop. She would get out,
adjust her sari and reach apartment blocks where memsaabs

would time her arrival. She would scrub and rinse utensils, swab the floor and wipe the furniture, windows and doors, house to house, in a relay. She would have her first meal of the day at one of the memsaabs' homes, seated unseen on the kitchen floor. At day-end, she would fight her way back home by a bus, a train and then the long meandering walk through narrow lanes of her shanty township. She would cook again and scrub and rinse at home as well and shout out for her children, who would trickle back in. Her husband, employed or not, would come home on the dot, hungry and thirsty for a drink or already drunk. He would ask for money if he did not have it and she would oblige without blinking or after a short-lived fight, knowing its end in advance. If in the mood, he would hit her or rape her or both. She would scream and cry or just shrug herself into a dreamless sleep. To wake up next day when the alarm rang.

Kaveri was lucky. Her husband had left her and her daughter Reshma was old enough to line up for water, cook and take care of their room. But Reshma did not take the train, preferring other ways to make a living. After Kaveri would leave for work, Reshma would splay for men and some women, most of whom would pay her for the largesse. Once a man had paid by punching her till she had bled from the mouth. She had not taken the infliction personally but requested one of her patrons, a local thug, to slash that man's throat. The thug had improvised and thrown the body into what was once a river and now a toxic nullah pumped with industrial effluents, muck and feces. The body was fished out a day later, a case was duly filed and duly forgotten.

Her mother endorsed Reshma's line of work for it did not involve sub-human public transport or the ceaseless toil of making a living unto death. It also earned them respect from the right people. But she was too old to start now.

Kaveri had made forty thousand rupees from the foolish memsaabs and maids of the Lalbaug tower, as a high-rise is referred to in her circle. It required a few sessions of sobbing and working on the egos of the maids who could still afford to live in the city. She had enjoyed milking them and had even parted with her real address, knowing none would trudge all the way to Nala Sopara even for a day to find her among crowds over a few thousands.

🌿

Susheela was among the few maids who actually owned a two-hundred-and-twenty-five-square-foot flat in Lalbaug where she had moved from a one-room home in a chawl.

She had shifted to the flat with her husband Kishor, son Suraj and sister-in-law Deepa who she married off in no time. Her parents-in-law had passed on before the flat was ready for possession.

All flats came with attached washrooms that made the residents wonder how they had ever queued up at public lavatories all these years.

Kishor did as Susheela directed, even though it was he who brought home most of the money. He did not drink, use abusive language or rape Susheela. He allowed her to abort her second pregnancy as she did not want an extra headache. He was a mythical creature in the neighbourhood whose wife talked down to him and he listened without hitting her. They had fought only once during their many years of marriage when he had slapped her and she had fainted, her hands stiffening in mimic rigor mortis. When she had revived, Susheela had found herself in a hospital and her husband bawling so loudly that the nurses had tittered. 'What kind of a wimp is he?' they had asked.

✤

After handing over the money, Aruna discussed Subodh's visit with Susheela who resumed crying with increased stamina.

'Madam, I think he wants to patch up with you,' she said, hiccupping for effect.

'He just came to convey his brother's death and that too after all the rites were over. The brother died last week. He did not call then,' Aruna reasoned.

'He could have called but he came.'

'He is the type that delivers bad news first-hand.'

Aruna grinned at Susheela's hope of seeing her generous employers, who did not cut her salary for missing work, reunited. Susheela's fondness was born out of ten long years of pleasant service. People get used to easy-going people and mistake routine for affection.

Aruna would now have to withdraw money from the ATM to replenish her wallet. Kaveri had managed to inconvenience her as well.

Chapter 8

GOPALA WAS AT HIS HIGH-SCHOOL FRIEND JOHN'S miniature tea plantation in the high ranges of the Munnar hill station of Kerala. The two men were unmindful of two women harvesting tender tea leaves a few feet away. Both made a play for Gopala by talking and laughing loudly, intrigued as they were by this landowner whose prolonged celibacy had been mentioned by their boss to a relative in their presence before the man himself had turned up.

The women discussed his slight built later. He was smaller than most men of his stature. The fall of his pants hinted at bow legs. His elbows jutted out at an angle from his half-sleeved shirt. His eyes were an irregular tawny with brown flecks that reflected the mixed parentage of coastal people and sat at odds with his strikingly unlined dark oval face. No one would call him handsome but women wanted to know him.

Gopala looked at one of the two workers without seeing her. She did not know that and fidgeted under the plastic wrap draped over her shirt that covered her saree, both kept in place with hemp twine. She began to vigorously pull at a tea shoot, pluck out the flushes and throw the tender buds into the wicker basket strapped to her back. She smiled self-consciously and looked down and then looked up only to notice Gopala had moved under a large silver oak that shaded a clump of tea bushes. His one hand, holding a cellphone, had reached out to the clouds in an obvious attempt to capture the mobile network. He wanted to connect with Mynah.

The woman, in bloom like the bushes around her, her three children left behind at home with accommodating in-laws for she made a decent income, now frowned as her expectations were dashed. But Gopala was blind to her and her dashed expectations, as he was to the teasing purple orchids and the wild cluster of pink rhododendrons close at hand which in his youth had evoked yearnings he had later systematically trained himself to kill. He did not smell the perfume of eucalyptus or the therapeutic wintergreen that filled the air either. He was deaf to the scurrying of a giant squirrel and to the crackling of leaves underneath a passing camera-shy Nilgiri tahr, majestic with its crown of curved horns and deadened grey eyes. He was equally indifferent to the whistling thrush and the bulbul's twang. This time, even the lush carpet of tea shrubs that had drawn him over the years to John's five-acre hobby plantation, the produce of which was gift-wrapped for guests, failed to cheer Gopala. He was visiting John's dying father in the dewy green mountains of Munnar that kept itself separate from the rest of coal-hot Kerala. Gopala forgot to shiver as icy winds cut through his skin. He was counting the hours before uninterrupted network would permit him to follow Mynah uninterruptedly.

If she were with him, she would have laughed happily while chattering away about her friends and studies and teachers. Her curls would have caught the sun and her large, expressive eyes, so like his, would have mirrored her father's contentment.

Gopala's pathological preoccupation with Mynah was natural. He was simulating his mother's investment in him, also an only child.

Gopala's mother Shaila was numb with shock when blessed with a full-term pregnancy and a child, a precious boy at that, in her forties, twenty-two years after her wedding. Shaila was a regal-looking big-boned woman with a sturdy frame and enormous breasts. The infant had struggled to latch on to a massive nipple at first, for he was exceptionally tiny at just a kilo and half at birth.

Gopala's father, Cyriac of Nilambur, like Subodh of Mumbai, was tormented by his fruitless member. He would squirm whenever cousins and uncles would cozy up to him to inquire about his health in the unsubtle hope of bagging something of his inheritance in the absence of an offspring. But what he did not notice for a long time was his wife's growing closeness to her maternal cousin, Romu, who was put in charge of the house whenever Cyriac had to travel. He returned one day to laughter that did not ring right. Maddened by his impotence, Cyriac kicked the cousin out with warnings of a wretched afterlife and went on to mount Shaila for the first time in bright afternoon and not at night with the lights off. From that day, Cyriac marked his territory often, which made Shaila fall in love with him rapidly and forget a heartbroken Romu. She showered her husband with genuine affection and he even began to touch her monstrous breasts, if tentatively at first. Love worked as a plastic surgeon.

⁂

The day Cyriac had first visited Shaila's place with his father and his maternal uncle with a marriage proposal, he had shyly looked her up and down and found her large but had been unable to gauge her mammoth bosom, hidden as it was behind a strategically pleated saree. Shaila had come with twenty kilograms of gold and twenty acres of land as dowry, which had made her persona appear demure to Cyriac's family. If it hadn't been for Romu and his dalliance with Shaila, Cyriac would not have had the opportunity of welcoming his son after eight years of renewed conjugal harmony. He had lifted his minuscule child in the nursing home for the first time with large tears and kissed him senseless.

Gopala was like Shaila in mannerism and approach. His refusal to move on after Gracy was symptomatic of their bullheadedness. Cyriac had pleaded with him and raged at him for not remarrying but had died bitter at his son's obstinacy. But Shaila, whose body had lost a little of its mass with age but not her will, was happy to have her son to herself in her widowhood and, as a bonus, a toy of a grandchild. After Cyriac's death following a heart attack, she had begun to openly thwart potential candidates for Gopala at engagements, weddings, children's naming ceremonies, funerals and post-death events—functions where families meet, exchange trivial, critical or scandalous information, and vend marital prospectives. Shaila progressively avoided social events altogether citing her advanced age, inadvertently narrowing the social circle of her son and granddaughter for they did not like to leave her alone at home. But invites never stop for people with means.

Chapter 9

RAM, FATHER OF THE GENTLEMANLY ROHIT WHO HAD joined a drenched Mynah in the Jamuna Heights elevator that rainy evening, had spent a major part of his life offering mathematics tuitions to children of people with means. He would walk an hour from his college where he taught the subject till one in the afternoon, to reach the residence of a student who wanted to become an accomplished pupil under his guidance. After an hour there, Ram would walk forty-five minutes to the next home, walk twenty minutes to the one thereafter and clamber on to a public transport bus to reach the last one, a half-hour ride away. He would reach home after dark. The next morning, before daybreak, he would queue up for milk at a kiosk to save on home delivery charges. He would return home, boil the unpasteurised milk and prepare tea for Radha, his wife, on a fuel-saving copper-bottom steel pan and wake her. She would mechanically curse him for delaying Rohit and Mohit, their sons named like a childish rhyme, for school. Ram would not even raise his eyes in response as harsh words and physical assault were the norm in his home. He would get ready to leave home by six-thirty and Radha would simultaneously tie her hair into a loose bun and get on with readying the children to hand them over to Cycle Mama, a middle-aged man whose job was to ferry them on his bicycle to school and back. She did not like the lowly task of dropping and picking up her children.

Rohit was older than Mohit by two years. His job as a child of five was to ensure Mohit's feet did not get entangled in the cycle's spokes, as he had seen happen to another child. Cycle Mama would ferry three children at a time. Two in front of him on spongy triangular seats with rexine covers and one behind on the mini steel luggage holder, Mohit's preferred spot. A little child had to sit sideways on the contraption as it was too wide. This was the same place where a girl from their school had sat dangling her legs and cried out in raw pain when her foot got caught in the rotating metal spokes of the back wheel. There were no more contenders for the seat thereafter and Mohit could just hop on, confident that his feet would never get caught in the wheel because his big brother was watching over him.

Rohit's early training in playing guardian made him meet life head-on while Mohit spent his childhood and then later years trying to match his brother in every department. Rohit went on to do what he wanted. He took up science. Mohit tried to do likewise but did not get admission for the course in a decent college, so he took up the next best option suggested by his parents—commerce. Mohit graduated and ended up joining his father's coaching institute as an administrator, a comfortable position from where he watched his brother's career as a landscape architect grow, first with admiration and then envy that turned into open jealousy as he himself gained in years and weight and little else. He was more of a dreamer like his mother than a practical man of action like his father and Rohit. If Mohit had been born first, he might have at least existed as his own person. He lost out to sequence.

But both brothers were blessed in equal measure with toughened genes, the only real inheritance of an impoverished ancestry. Ram's father, Shankarbhai, was a temple priest back home in the green city of Junagadh, near the Asiatic lion forest reserve of Gir, towards the west of the western state of Gujarat. Shankarbhai specialised in conducting weddings and naming ceremonies. He had wanted Ram, a good student, to leave for Mumbai and carve out a life in a modern world. Ram reached Mumbai and did his Bachelor of Education, the degree required to teach, and landed a job in a college. The salary adequately paid for the rent of a room in a chawl in Bhuleshwar—an old, crumbling locality to the city's south famous for its great many temples. Around two years after marriage, he upgraded to a one-bedroom flat in Dahisar, the northern-most suburb. He sent his children to an English medium school there, where they wore ties and canvas shoes with laces, a matter of pride for him but not for Radha.

She did not like being tucked away in far-off Dahisar. The beauteous girl with straight dark brown hair, clear green eyes, an aquiline nose and plump pink lips, had agreed to an arranged match with the lacklustre Ram for the allure of the city of gold. Bombay to her was where people moved about in Premier Padminis and Maruti 800s and women wore sunglasses and pants. The alliance was meant to be an indescribable improvement over her little home in her hometown of Rajkot in Gujarat, some distance from Junagadh. Disappointed in the wimp of a husband whom she hit easily in frustration when her dream of relocating to a less impoverished space was broken, she drilled into her sons the value of aspiration. She underscored that their neighbours were not worth interacting with, the place where they lived was dirtier than a village, not the Bombay that people spoke of with awe—the land couched within an azure sea, where people saw off the sun at a C-shaped Marine Drive or at the long linear stretch of Juhu beach, the location home to mythical film stars who partied endlessly. She had stared at the vision without blinking while watching Hindi movies and reading Gujarati movie magazines, and the idea of replaying it for herself had taken form. It made her pray fervently for a release from her parents' two-room house with an outdoor kitchen shaded with a straw roof under which she had to blow into a long wooden hollow tube to fan the flames of firewood and dried dung cakes. Radha would place aluminium cooking pots on the earthen stove, squint her eyes as smoke made them smart, and then sit back and daydream.

Her father, Ghelabhai, would occasionally accompany Ram's uncle, Shyamjibhai, to ceremonies. It was Shyamjibhai who had villainously arranged her marriage and what she had erroneously thought of as her escape from poverty. The sole respite she got through the arrangement was from blowing at recalcitrant flames, collecting firewood and dung, and chewing on neem sticks to clean her teeth.

Radha had smiled shyly at Ram and made all the right moves and sounds when intimate with him after the wedding, in his likewise two-room home in Junagadh. She had left for the city a few days later on a train, smiling at Ram but looking past his eyes. Beaming, she had gotten off at Bombay Central station and stepped into the city, right foot first. The couple had boarded a taxi and Ram had asked the driver to take a detour to show his wife unimaginably grand buildings constructed in neo-Gothic, Art Deco, Indo-Saracenic, traditional and current styles. They did not stop in front of any on their way home. The couple got out outside an alley and walked some way till Ram turned to his right and they entered a pitch-black space. Radha stumbled a little and held on to her husband, her heart pounding in anticipation. They walked on till he opened a door and felt a wall to hunt down a switch. When the light came on, Radha found herself in a musty room. There was a single iron cot on one side and a raised kitchen platform opposite. An open trunk on the floor served as a wardrobe. A space separated by a half-wall next to the kitchen served as the bathroom.

The room reeked of age. The wooden staircase outside creaked each time someone jumped over a missing step. Ram's room was on the first floor, one among innumerable others in the four-storey chawl where even sunlight refused to enter. It was built next to an exposed drain where residents freely discarded their garbage. It bubbled with sub-aquatic life and insects, and smelly waters flooded the entrance to the chawl after merely an hour of rain.

Radha crouched on the bed and cried till sleep rendered her temporarily dead. She woke up to curse Ram, his uncle and her parents and hoped they got festering boils on their behinds, contracted cancer and suffered a painful death.

When Ram announced their move to a flat in Dahisar, a year after Rohit's birth, Radha felt like herself again. She hugged him and let him fondle her without squirming. Mohit was a product of this patchwork coupling. They had a few months of peace, and then Radha understood she had been short-changed. She learnt that Dahisar back in the 1990s was little different from Rajkot. Both were small towns with poor quality apartments.

That night when Ram had inched close, she had pushed him away with such force that he had fallen off the new plywood bed with wooden-finish Sunmica selected by Radha during her short-lived effervescent phase.

Radha would now access him for money and the only physical contact would be her hand on his body when she attacked him. The first time she slapped him was a year into their marriage, when Rohit was two months old. She had then looked around and picked up a stick used to put up clothes to dry on a string outside their room. She had beaten him till he had pleaded for his life, and then thrown the stick and herself on the floor. She had wept so copiously and with such truth that Ram had felt empathy well up for her disappointment in him. He wanted to apologise to her but feared for his life. Besides, Rohit was bawling in his crib for an end to the nuisance.

When she had stopped sobbing, she had screamed at Ram in a hoarse voice, 'You dog. You eunuch. When you did not have the capacity to get married, why did you even come to my place? Where did you find the confidence to land up at my door, you two-bit cheat? Look at me. I should have been in a bungalow. That was what I was born for. Not this shithole. Do you understand?'

Ram had sat on the floor, hand on his forehead, with

regret at his inability to make his woman love him. He did not love her either. But she was given to him in marriage and marriages had to last. She was right. He had brought her to the city with nothing to offer but thwarted ambition.

Radha never let go of an opportunity to abuse Ram in front of her sons who copied their mother's disrespect of him. She spent her life imagining what could have been while lying on a bed that was too small for two.

Chapter 10

ARUNA ASKED SUSHEELA TO HELP LIFT MYNAH OUT OF bed and Susheela asked Aruna to be allowed to accompany the two in a taxi called inside the complex compound by security guards. As they entered the elevator, Raja, the liftman, smirked at the scene of devastation that Mynah's face was and at the two older women holding her vertical.

The trio clumsily got into the taxi and exited the complex to drive past the dwindling chawls of Lalbaug that had once also housed textile mills for over a century.

⁂

Just as a spark is all that it takes to set off a blaze, after the brick-laying ceremony of Bombay's very first textile mill in 1851, fifty-three more sprang up swathing over a thousand acres of free land in central Sewri, Prabhadevi, Byculla, Mazagaon, Reay Road and Parel, to which Lalbaug belongs or is a sister zone—a matter of optics. In the late eighteenth century, Parel housed the official home of a governor of Bombay. It was later shifted south to a fifty-acre lush spread called Raj Bhavan where peacocks still roam and dance as they please.

The mills were strategically constructed a few kilometres from Fort—the only noteworthy hub of commerce then—and did much to embellish the city's reputation as the country's foremost wealth creator. Girangaon, as the midtown village of mills was called, went on to employ close to three-quarters of Mumbai's labour force by the early half of the twentieth century.

The end of the boom came unannounced and swiftly in the early 1980s, following a standoff between obdurate mill owners and determined labour unions over bonuses. The labour strike extended for eighteen months and snapped the industry's backbone.

Some mills outside the city benefited from the mass closure as a number of quicksilver workers moved there. But the majority that numbered lakhs stayed on, and hopefully and then hopelessly watched padlocks on large iron doors of mill compounds rust and the land and structures within disappear and disintegrate under the musty foliage of disuse. They were caught in a bottomless vortex of penury as the strike was the biggest in the world in terms of the number of strikers involved and the longest, although it was never declared officially over. Its catastrophic scale saw the cottonopolis sink and hasten the city's deindustrialisation.

It was over two years since Mynah's interview at Ad Grande in 2017.

The two-storey chawl right outside Jamuna Heights that the three women were passing was topped with Mangalore tiles and each floor was lined with a balcony along a common corridor supported by wooden railings and thin balusters where a few blank-faced men stood in white vests, brown shorts and towels casually flung over their shoulders, looking on at the happenings on the road below. This chawl, which housed former mill workers' families, was awaiting a builder to be redeveloped. Perhaps it was caught in litigation or recession that had depressed the property market since the end of the new millennium's first decade.

Jamuna Heights had come up where a desolate mill once was. It had been flattened and the debris carted off in dusty, rickety trucks. A large chunk of the locked mill land in the city had been sold to developers.

Subodh had bought a flat in the complex for a steal in 2007, for the locality, though central, had then carried a working-class tag. As land rates can only rise in a sea-framed city, twelve years hence, the complex was occupied by mostly wealthy businessmen, traders and senior corporate executives who wished to live in a gated community with facilities that older, entrenched locations could not offer considering the premium every square foot commanded there.

The more modern apartment blocks offered multiple parking lots, valets to park vehicles, Olympic-sized in-house pools, tennis and squash courts, jogging tracks and skating rinks, and parks for children to play in and one for pets to frolic and poop in too. Since Jamuna Heights was of a decade-old vintage, it had to make do with a regular pool and a vanilla clubhouse with a community hall mostly patronised by the complex's retired residents. Its gymnasium overlooked a lawn, a walking track and the artificially grown forest, barring the original banyan. Not only did the builders not cut the holy tree while developing the plot, they even built a temple beside it.

It was August-end and five days to Ganeshotsav, the annual ten-day community festival when idols of the elephant-headed Lord Ganesha are installed at hundreds of marquees across the city. At festival-end, the idols are immersed in water by the teary devout who exhort the lord to speed up his return the following year. Two of the grandest marquees in the city for the festival were near Jamuna Heights.

The organisers of one of the venues were bustling about. Senior members were making arrangements for lighting and entertainment programmes, and to keep track of astronomical public donations that pour in for the festival.

Each marquee boasts a specific current affairs theme since spreading awareness about social issues is normative during Ganeshotsav, for Ganesha himself is the God of Wisdom.

The decoration around the idol, carved out of thermocol and wood, was being given finishing touches with gold and red spray paint by the many artistes. Uniformed security men were guarding the marquee to make certain that the theme did not become public until the grand unveiling of the idol. The watchful guards were glaring at passers-by and passing vehicles with self-importance and suspicion endemic to their occupation.

As the taxi with Mynah and her wards snaked its way through the narrow lane partially cordoned off for the marquee, one of the guards in charge of keeping the curious out peered inside the vehicle and lost interest on seeing three women. The taxi passed on to the main street past archaic shops that are now seen in few other places in the city. The dated markets served the original families of the locality as a time-honoured routine that countered the threat of an alien, changing neighbourhood.

Some of the shop boards displayed wistful names that included the word 'Worker' in the local Marathi language. These shops sold everything but textiles. On the opposite end was one with a traditional Indian name which weighed tobacco leaves by the gram on a ferrous machine that had not been permitted to rust. The shrivelled owner of the establishment sat on a stool opposite the weighing machine and sliced betel nuts with an oversized metal cutter, a smile playing on his chapped lips, perhaps because there was no anti-tobacco message with grotesque faces of death pasted on his shop board. Next to it was a stall where knives and scissors were being sharpened against a large motorised iron wheel, sending out querulous sparks upon metal-on-metal contact. Alongside were other stalls that looked angrier, for they had on display large open jute sacks filled with spices—fiery whole red chillies, both fleshy and shrivelled, plonked alongside dried pungent turmeric roots, whole asafoetida, and coriander and caraway seeds. Owners of a spice business have no need to cover the spice bags or for pest control. No insect dares venture near these bags for fear of being scorched, maimed or annihilated by the condiments.

In the tiny lane perpendicular to the spice shop, not visible from the taxi, stood a long line of shops that specialised in chips and not just of potato. They also sold crispy slivers of salted raw banana and umami yam and elephant root, and a snacky savoury sweet-sour mixture of puffed rice, deep fried lentil vermicelli, raisins, peanuts and cashew, all of which were tossed together and subjected to a tempering of fresh curry leaves, mustard seeds and chillies in sizzling vegetable oil, topped with a squeeze of tangy lime.

On the road where the taxi was waiting at a red signal

several stores vended ready-to-wear festive traditional nine-yard sarees of Maharashtra and chaniya cholis from Gujarat for women aged zero to a hundred and three, as a salesman was shouting to bring in customers. Right next to it was an array of shops with stacks of cloth in a thousand colours, to be rolled up like ropes and wound around heads. The quickly created turbans would proudly declare the community to which their wearers belonged during marriages and festivals, for each ties the headgear differently and in distinct shades.

A little away temporary stalls called attention to resplendent idols of Goddess Gauri, Ganesha's mother, for she too is worshipped during the festival alongside her son. For prayer reasons again, there were shops that sold large banana stalks to serve as propitious beams at two ends of entry gates at special functions to welcome guests. More stalls sold other prayer-ware—lamps, wicks and camphor balls that give out cool vapours when lit, matches to ignite them with, fragrance sticks in rose, sandalwood and jasmine, plastic flower garlands that negate the need to dispose of fresh ones at day-end, tiny and large sugar balls, thin transparent oblong sugar slices and puffed rice to be distributed as edible offerings, lots of vermillion and turmeric powder, and white and red sandalwood to be moistened and rubbed against a marble pestle till it turns into a paste that must be scooped with the auspicious finger of the right hand and rubbed against the forehead.

Mynah cherished her visits to this crowded market with Aruna and then Rohit in the evenings, and the jostling the stroll offered. She had pointed out to Aruna how incongruous the market seemed to outsiders like herself in a most modern city and how harmoniously it co-existed with malls in the physical world and shopping destinations in the virtual. She hoped this quaint treasure would not be demolished to make space for yet another faceless shopping plaza.

Mynah would wind up her walk by passing a fire temple and stepping into a dargah, hidden behind a rising high-rise near the market. She would stand still for a while, trying to tune out the grind of construction work and its dust that caught inside the pores of her skin and made her eyes smart.

The sun made Mynah squint. She did not feel Aruna's soft shoulder on which her head lay, right under the afternoon glare. She was as indifferent to Susheela's calloused hand on her thigh.

Unlike her companions, a life-hardened Susheela's senses were always on the alert to the physical world, its threats and promises. Amid the gloom that had darkened the taxi and depressed the driver who wanted the women to get off as quickly as it could be managed so that he could get on with feeling upbeat again, Susheela easily noticed a mill of another kind at yet another red signal. It was a two hundred-square-foot flour and spice mill where three customers had lined up. They were watching the transformation of wheat, sorghum, rice and corn kernels into flour and pounding of spices without blinking, not trusting the miller to return the quality raw material they had handed to him in large aluminium dabbas or the original weight. Susheela remembered she had to stock up on the annual supply of essentials, for buying these at one go was cheaper than picking things up as and when. She would mix some castor oil as a natural preservative into the rice and whole lentils to keep out the crawlies. The pest-proof spices would be mixed and powdered at the mill to a consistency to suit her family's personalized taste—a compromise couples reach after years of cohabitation, both parties having grown in homes with their own individual taste in food, the status quo arrived at after a textbook power struggle.

This masala would be generously dunked into gravies.

In her head, where things really take place, Susheela was at home, preparing a fragrant chicken curry without water, the meat cooking in its own juices and spices powdered at the mill. The aroma was so powerful that it blasted into the homes of jealous neighbours, two of whom landed at her place to find out what was being cooked.

'So, Susheela, what's today's special?' asked one.

'Just a simple chicken curry with the masala I got powdered last year. I still have a bottle of it left. My husband bought chicken from the Sunday bazaar,' said Susheela, her nostrils flaring with pride at the economic weight of her statement. Its effect was not lost on her friends.

'How many kilos?' asked the same woman.

'One and a half. He was a fat fellow,' said Susheela, her tongue caressing her inner right cheek in its wayward arrogance. Too late, she thought. They would dissect her fat chicken story for days.

The women smiled at the supposed joke.

'What are you two preparing today?' Susheela asked them.

One replied, 'Just sardine. You know we had to spend five hundred rupees on the ceiling's repair work. But the leakage has still not stopped. That bitch on top from whose bathroom floor the water keeps dripping into ours and makes that maddening tip-tip sound will not pay even a rupee for the plumbing. The last two times, we had to shell out every single paisa for the repairs, but we have now decided to not keep quiet. I will pull out her panties and beat her up till she lands in hospital.'

'But don't do it today. I've got guests coming over,' said Susheela, who enjoyed her own jokes.

'Who's coming?' asked the one who was more inquisitive of the two.

'Kusum aunty,' said Susheela, making a face.

'Alone?'

'No, no. With that obese daughter-in-law and her matchstick children. I think she eats up all their food. I'm going to ensure the kids are at least fed well in my house.'

'They'll be here for how long?'

'Just for lunch. I'll see to it they are packed off before our TV serial starts at five. You remember, right? Today we will find out if Shom and Khushi manage to tell her parents of her pregnancy. Those kids will not sit quiet and I won't have time to watch the re-rerun tomorrow morning. I'll be at work then.'

'Yes, you must come up with some excuse. Why does she keep coming here? For free food? Such a lowly person.'

Susheela and her neighbours had no boundaries. Open doors were the norm and conversations got personal without introduction. Even new residents ended up commenting on personal stuff without self-consciousness or embarrassment. The concept of yours and mine had no space in slums and chawls where people lived in a crush. The tradition carried forward in buildings where former mill workers' families were provided accommodation through a lottery. Every discussion in every home was known, transmitted, commented upon and judged.

Chapter 11

SUSHEELA'S FATHER-IN-LAW KRISHNA COULD NOT HEAR his neighbours while crouching in the sole uncluttered corner of his one-room home that resembled a discarded doll house with its grey walls. His face was an ashen, leathery grid of strife and his legs spindly knobs as he sat on his haunches. His bony hands were placed lightly on his knees. His rheumy eyes were yellowed and his hearing was a mournful reminiscence.

As a boy he could hear as well as anyone around him. The constant roar of machines in the two decades he had spent in the spinning department of a textile mill had ruptured his eardrums. He now responded to mime while living out his silent days.

He would often think of his first few years in the big city, sleeping in a single room with twenty textile workers, with no space to even turn. But Krishna, who had a happy constitution and for whom life was a string of moments that held no greater significance than his experience of them, never let himself forget that he was among the privileged who had a room to sleep in. His friends and colleagues from the Konkan and the Ghat regions of Maharashtra, and others from the states of Uttar Pradesh up north and Tamil Nadu and Telangana down south spent their nights on the road outside, waiting for a vacancy to crop up inside.

He worked three shifts. On his way to work and back, he would be invigorated by typical smells and sounds— cooking of food and crackling of masala from the community kitchens, the pleasurably suffocating odour of roasting of tobacco and frying of dried fish from homes, shout-outs of vendors of onion, garlic, areca nut and multi-coloured glass bangles, and smoke of lit bidis.

If at home in the afternoon, his siesta would be broken by raucous jugglers with topi-wearing monkeys. Krishna's favourite, though, was the bioscope man permanently stationed next to his regular tea stall. The contraption's primitive manual projector boasted five viewing rounds that allowed him a dekko at electric bulb-lit colour reels and frames of foremost tourist hotpots and movie stars.

Some days, the lane outside his room would quiver from the lashings that members of the Potraj tribe would give themselves. Associated with the myth of Kadaklakshmi, a deity who remedies ailments, they would turn up in groups of three or four, their sunburnt foreheads smeared with dramatic vermilion red, turmeric yellow and ash. Krishna would unfailingly hand over two-paise coins to them and fold his hands to seek their blessings.

He would avidly await performances of myriad art forms that grew around him—naman that would start with a prayer and a bow, the dashavtar theatre of epics, and the devotional bharud and lalit.

Some evenings, Krishna would land up to watch the rustic bahurangi tamasha performances at Hanuman Theatre, one of the six near his chawl. He would nod along as on stage men and women—dressed in nine-yard zari sarees and loaded with heavy jewellery and makeup—would sing, dance and intersperse their act with unscripted dialogue in simple language that he grasped and appreciated.

Folk plays would be performed on temporary stages set up on cordoned-off streets. Between the acts of plays, political speeches would be made after the speakers were received effusively with thunderous claps and firecrackers.

The vibrancy that mill workers lent to their social lives seeped into the cultural ethos of the city. The Communists who dominated trade unions had a tangible influence on the cultural profile of the microcosm of mill areas as well. The Progressive Writers' Movement and the Indian People's Theatre Association flourished. Parel became the centre of Left literature and theatre. The Communist Party of India hosted discourses, think-tanks and brainstormers on national and international issues, usually of an economic nature.

Though satisfied with their social life, most of Krishna's

friends, unlike him, hoped for better pay. Gymnasiums and traditional wrestling joints of kushti akharas with floors of brick red medicinal mud were where workers clandestinely met political activists and trade union leaders to air complaints. Akharas were also used for their muscle power and to secure the success of a strike and frighten blacklegs into falling in line. Much blood was spilt during the final strike and top union leaders and workers were killed.

The feeling of want among the workers was further fuelled by strident political speeches during cultural events and wrenching ballads of Left-leaning shahirs, people's poet-singers.

   Where the Communists fell short, though, was on their sole focus on class-related issues in their zeal to unite workers. These global concerns did not resonate with the workers on a personal level—their anxieties about jobs and religious and caste beliefs. Marathi-speaking workers, who formed the majority of the labour class, gravitated to a nascent Shiv Sena, a local party supported by the national Congress. The Sena filled the vacuum by speaking the workers' language and projecting their regional pride, which ultimately led to the weakening of the Communist base and labour movement in the city.

Workers' lives were cleaved into periods before the strike and afterwards. They could not hope to land their lost jobs but wanted a little piece of the land on which they had toiled before.

They marched and moved courts for it. An apolitical and docile Krishna, who went along on marches to fill his empty days, was one of the twenty thousand workers and their families among close to two lakh applicants to be allotted flats in buildings built for them over long decades.

Krishna's mortal self did not see his flat nor did his wife, a professional cook. His son, daughter and daughter-in-law joyously did.

Krishna's body was found leaning against the thin walls of his chawl room, his eyes vacantly looking forward to making peace with his death.

Chapter 12

Radha's denouncement of her neighbours in the Bhuleshwar chawl was delivered to them through porous walls and rendered her a recluse. It did not make a dent in her disgust for them though. The neighbours would taunt her when she would pass by on her way in or out, for that was the only time they saw her. She did not heed them.

If she had, they would have fought with her, and even this fractious engagement would have offered her an escape from self-imposed loneliness.

They would have shared their untutored anger with her and then, at some later date, the intimacy generated by the antagonism might have led to a patch-up.

Radha and her children did not know of equations in their wholesomeness, in lack of transactions, of uncomplicated give and take, the bear hug that mammals need. She had shut out that primal requirement like an ostrich who hides her head deep in a self-created hole. The mother and sons spent days and nights investing in a future that was not allowed to percolate into the present. Radha stood a loser in the bargain and spent a lifetime not knowing it. She passed on the dissatisfaction with her quasi life to her sons who were always impoverished in their heads, always wanting, never getting, and if they got something, they stopped wanting it because by being theirs the thing had somehow degraded itself.

One of Radha's children had managed to scald Mynah.

From the angle at which Mynah lay her head on Aruna's shoulder, she saw the grey-blue polluted sky. Cirrus clouds were flying past and purposeful birds were flapping their wings. It was going-home time for the avians and Mynah was speeding away from hers. The sun hurt her eyes and she clapped them shut with one hand. She had always felt light amplify during examinations and then on result days and at that point in the taxi. Such days of too much light that made people feel woozy should be called Sundays, she had told Gopala once, who found everything Baby uttered riveting.

The taxi climbed onto a flyover that obliterated the world beneath but for a geriatric chimney to its right. A wedge in the grey cobblestone chimney had sprouted a sapling.

From the flyover, the occupants of the taxi could not have seen an urchin stepping into a forlorn shed in this mill compound. The deserted space and its mouldy but harmless walls were inviting to an insecure child who had seen no better. The guards who were told to be present at all times to report trespassing were away for tea, leaving the gate ajar. The boy ventured to lie undisturbed in the square shed. A few hours later, the same guards berated the boy on seeing him exit the gate. He ran and melted into the crowd.

As wind hit her face in the moving vehicle, Susheela thought of Suraj and felt her eyes moisten. He had been the brightest pupil at school. She and Kishor did not have to pay his fees for he was a scholarship student. He stood first in the state board exam in his English medium school, the only child among Susheela's friends to go to one. The celebrations and distribution of sweets went on for weeks. When he secured admission to St Xavier's College near Fort, Susheela gave him a teaspoon of the auspicious sweetened curd and milk, kissed his right cheek and told him to study well and appear for his medical entrance after the two-year course to become a doctor, one of the top two dreams that Indian parents harbour for their children, the other being engineer. Aruna and the other memsaabs for whom Susheela worked told her of the procedure to sit for the tests and each gave their blessings and a hundred and one rupees for good luck. By the time Suraj reached his second and final year of junior college, he began to play cricket in a public ground near his residence. He was mesmerized by the game and spoke of becoming a cricketer like the greats his city had produced. One day he told his shocked parents he would follow his heart, not theirs, and signed up for cricket coaching. Studies took a backseat.

He failed junior college and did not even get selected into a local cricket team.

A broken Suraj quit both college and cricket. He stopped stepping out of home and slept for hours. His parents lost face among neighbours and relatives, who relished the fall of the local hero. But after a year, even they began to worry for him and one Tuesday, the special day of the week to pray to Ganesha, they walked from their homes, some fifty of them, to the Lord's wish-fulfilling Siddhivinayak temple a few kilometres from their home.

They broke coconuts and made offerings of marigold garlands to the deity after queuing up in a kilometre-long line with thousands of others like them for two hours to enter the shrine. Once in, they prayed to Ganesha to imbue life back into their Suraj.

Two days later, Suraj went out for an evening walk. The third day, a neighbour got him a job offer as a waiter at a pub in Parel, not far from home. He stared at Suraj, heart pounding, for a positive reaction. It came in the form of an affirmative nod. The entire neighbourhood celebrated that day the way they had done when he had topped his school.

His parents and neighbours sat on the floor of the kitchen of their flat to roll out and roast a sweet and soft bread of wheat, lentils, jaggery and pure cow ghee, and offered plate upon plate of it with cups of saffron milk to whoever came visiting to wish them luck. The same team that had visited the temple once again landed in front of the idol and thanked him profusely, this time bright-eyed.

Chapter 13

Suraj, krishna's grandson, was at the pub where he had become a senior waiter after two years of service. He made close to twenty-five thousand rupees a month, enough to get by, considering he lived with his parents and had no plans or wherewithal to purchase or rent a home of his own.

The pub was located in a less redeveloped mill land opposite a prosperous one that housed an upper-crust mall, a five-star hotel, a clutch of fine-dine and quirky new-age restaurants, cafes and pubs where the young laughed and drank and swayed and danced. The floor below these spaces that played loud music had turned deaf decades ago, like Krishna, due to the clangour of textile machinery.

Now, the progeny of a few of the mill workers worked in the new businesses that had sprung up like shoots in spring after an interminable cold spell.

꽃

Sometimes when Suraj was beginning his work day or winding up at the end of one at a reconstructed space, before or after the woofers had been plugged out, he heard sounds that sounded familiar to him. He was at the pub housed inside a shed, unit number twenty-four, in the former mill compound, a short bus ride towards the west from his home and Mynah's paying guest digs. The place, run by a Louisiana State University graduate who had returned from the US after losing his job to the 2008 recession, sat oddly next to unit number twenty-one, a three-thousand-square-foot empty space that was yet to find a lessee. During his breaks, Suraj often stepped inside the unlit interiors that stank of rubble and rusted iron but was good enough to light up unseen and undisturbed. The shed was doorless as there was nothing left to steal.

The north-light facing glazed roof of this structure that had been used to store cans of dyes was so high that the owner was looking to give it out to a pub for the echo effect a large cavernous space naturally offers. The two-storey building opposite the sheds was tougher and stood on cast-iron columns. It had been chopped into multiple chunks that were rented out as offices and art studios, with ugly, dripping rears of air-conditioners jutting out of their closely partitioned windows. The interiors where office-goers now sat had once accommodated heavy machinery. Next to the tall structure was a square tower block used as a dust chimney and alongside rose a long and large funnelling chimney from where no smoke had escaped for a generation.

The offices were quiet as the staff had left for the day. The compound was yet to fill with the after-hours crowd. As it was early in the day for the evening rush hour at the pub, Suraj headed out for a smoke inside the eerie unit number twenty-one at dusk.

Inside, his alert eyes followed the sound of a rodent's squeak that faded out near a wall at the other end of the endless room which curiously lit up to reveal two men dressed in brown. They clocked their entry time in a register kept at the table and walked towards a corner. One of them pulled at the lever of a monstrous machine that started with a reluctant but deafening roar. The machine scrunched into action, first a little rusty and then not. It caught speed and began to spin out reams of thread into cloth that flowed on to the floor and covered the rubble inch by inch, and then faster, foot by foot, and then metre by metre, till the entire square footage of the shed was covered by it. The cloth carpet looked a lot like his favourite bed sheet from childhood of pink and blue flowers. As a boy, he had thought of the bed sheet as a litmus paper experiment at school. After every wash, he expected the pink of the bed sheet to turn blue or the blue to pink, to find out if the washing powder was more acidic or alkaline. The cloth did not change colour. It faded with time.

Moments later, a siren sounded and the machines stopped, their silence deafening to his throbbing ears.

The workers walked to the canteen in another corner of this many-cornered place and took out their tiffins that revealed chappatis, dal, vegetables, rice and porridge of sago and peanuts. They ate without making chewing noises or exchanging work-spawned bonhomie. It was that quiet.

A rat ran over Suraj's foot, making him jump, lose his balance and trip over. He stood up in the dark and patted the dust off his trousers. As he walked out, the vision of his grandfather faded out.

Chapter 14

Harsha had come home to help Subodh pack and leave, smiling at Aruna who had responded with one of her own. She did not need to understand the game. His leaving her was a given. Her sole concern now was how to fill her days in the absence of a timetable.

Subodh had not wanted Harsha to accompany him but she had insisted on tagging along in her pyjamas, crumpled top and hair pulled back in a ponytail, making a statement of her unwashed morning body and bare face. Aruna was in a blouse and linen trousers that she put on to receive outsiders at home to make a good impression in a long line of good impressions. She had even lined her eyes with kohl to define the formality demanded of an occasion involving visitors.

'Would you like tea or coffee, Harsha?' asked Aruna, as expected of a good host.

'I've just had tea that Subodh made for me. He's such a sweetheart,' replied Harsha and looked fondly at him.

'Yes, he is,' said Aruna simply and was wondering what to

say next when Harsha asked, 'He used to make it for you?'

'No. Will you have anything else? This packing business will take a long time. Have you had breakfast?' Aruna went on, not liking the idea of sending back a guest unfed.

'Do you have a lady or a man cook?' asked Harsha.

'Neither. I'm old school, I guess. My parents never had the means to afford one so I learnt to cook early on. I must have been seven when I cooked dal in a pressure cooker for the first time. The cooker was half my size. My parents would leave for school in the morning—they were teachers and taught in the secondary section which had morning sessions. I would prepare lunch before I left for school by twelve as I was in the primary section then.'

'Twelve at noon?' asked Harsha.

Aruna laughed affably and nodded.

Harsha had stormed into an empty fort in an armour and then rushed to find a nook to put up a flag and wave at the applause from an audience that only the victor could see and hear.

Aruna had ceded her claim on Subodh the first time he had brought the first woman home. If he had told her of his indiscretions or demonstrated remorse, she would have fought for his affection. That he had chosen to flaunt his conquests shut her up.

When she was around fourteen, Aruna had heard a pup's feeble cry. She was alone in her ground-floor flat in Pune. Her parents were away and Suyash was out playing with friends. She had stepped out, concerned, to find the whimpering animal and rushed back inside to look for the chipped saucer that no one used or was likely to use but her mother had carefully stored in the kitchen cabinet for an emergency. 'What if the other saucers break?' her mother would ask them rhetorically. All the cabinets and the single loft in their one-bedroom flat were crammed with items for emergencies her mother hoarded. Whenever such an occasion arose, say, once in three years, she'd feel vindicated and look at her husband with a superior, I-told-you-so gaze. Aruna and Suyash would smile indulgently at their mother and forget about the incident, till the next emergency.

That day the brown saucer with the chipped edge that revealed a bit of its brittle creamy china skeleton did come in handy. Aruna filled it with milk and rushed out. The shivering pup slurped up the liquid within seconds and followed her inside for more. A moved Aruna lifted the animal to find that the pup was born neutered—it did not have a scrotum. A while later, Aruna heard the sound of yelps and went out to see the pup's family lodged under a shaded patch some distance away. It struck her that the pup had been deliberately left to die by its mother. Since her own mother was strictly anti-pets, she picked up the pup and dumped it next to the brood. The other pups were visibly excited to see their missing sibling but the mother looked away, almost human in her disdain. Aruna went home and shut the door to the animal whom she had supplied with short-term refuge, knowing it would die soon. She did not sleep well that night and hoped it would not curse her while exhaling its concluding breath.

A gloating Harsha, her guard habitually up, had spent a lifetime removed from maternal love like the impotent pup Aruna had rescued and then knowingly sent to its death. The death of Harsha's father when she was a year old was limited to the marking of a calendar for the annual prayer offerings for his soul. At the age of four, she was sent to the boarding school. The first few nights she had cried herself to sleep. Her classmates had become her foster family. The toddlers held hands and snuggled, often cold again on breaking of contact. The children eventually got used to timetables—waking at six, bathing by half past six, breakfast by eight, school at eight thirty, two breaks in between, release at four, play time from five, heading for music and dance class at seven, bathing again at eight, dinner at eight thirty, studying till nine thirty and switching off lights thereafter. But her life was not as structured and regimented as that of the maids of Nala Sopara or Ram, the college professor-cum-coaching-class-owner, because two days a week the students were taken out for field trips or given lessons in acting, and on weekends they watched movies in the common hall and kicked off a riot while doing so.

Harsha knew it in her bones that Malini didn't miss her. She spent her breaks with Malini and later with Malini and Madhav as an unwanted appendage. Both mother and stepfather brightened when it was time for her return to school. Malini hugged and kissed Harsha with more enthusiasm than when she turned up at home. The first evening of her arrival, Harsha would be paraded at the club. Harsha's visits were timed in an hourglass half-filled with yellowed sand. The time was always up when it was up and all were relieved for it.

Aruna's teacher parents spent school holidays and long breaks mostly lolling at home or at their siblings' homes in the city or friends' pads in the neighbourhood. They would take her and Suyash to the cold hill stations of Lonavla or Mahabaleshwar, not too far from home. The children would be dressed in cardigans and pullovers and their ears covered with woollen mufflers. The four looked forward to holidays the entire year.

Ambitious for their children, Aruna's parents sent the two to Mumbai, the country's economic nerve centre, after their schooling. A seventeen-year-old Suyash, an effortless student, studied medicine at Seth GS Medical College as a resident. Two years later, a seventeen-year-old Aruna was placed in a students' hostel in Colaba, close to HR College of Commerce at Churchgate in the south where she enrolled for three years and graduated with a first class. But she forgot most things she had learnt at school and college. To her, studies were a path to a career and career something to hold on to till she married.

After her second short-lived relationship, Aruna took a sabbatical from boyfriends. Subodh was a batch-mate but in another class. It was only in her third and final year of college that she met him between lectures.

They began to notice each other and found it difficult to exchange a smile or keep their hands from smoothening their hair into place or rubbing an earlobe when the other passed. One day Aruna went up to Subodh on seeing him alone and asked him to accompany her to the college canteen where they shared a vegetable sandwich.

She began to wait for him and he for her, their faces lighting up on spotting each other. They would walk along Marine Drive that lined the coast a few metres from their college and look for nooks. They had found something that mattered. She cherished it till he threw it away.

Subodh and Harsha left after hugging her in turns, the way the civilised discard the vulnerable.

Aruna waited till they got into the elevator, smiled and waved, shut the door and collapsed.

Chapter 15

Mʏɴᴀʜ ᴏᴘᴇɴᴇᴅ ᴛʜᴇ ᴅᴏᴏʀ ᴛᴏ ᴀʀᴜɴᴀ'ꜱ ᴅᴀʀᴋᴇɴᴇᴅ ꜰʟᴀᴛ with her key. She felt the switchboard for lights and called out while making her way to Aruna's room to find her in bed.

'Aunty, what's the matter? Are you unwell?' she asked, reaching for Aruna's forehead to check for temperature.

Aruna jerked awake and looked around with mad eyes, rubbed her face and asked Mynah for the time. When told, she guiltily rushed to the kitchen and heated up food. She was not alone and the thought lifted her.

Chapter 16

'SIR, WHY DO YOU WANT TO NAME YOUR DAUGHTER Mynah. You know the superstition around it,' Raman, Gopala's wizened estate manager, put forth tentatively.

'What superstition? I love the name. I've loved it since I was a child, though I personally don't really like the boring brown and black bird. It is certainly not like the parakeets that are so colourful—blue, red, yellow, green, pink. But then, mynah does have lovely yellow-rimmed black eyes. I and Baby have yellow eyes with black eyelashes. That is our one big similarity with the bird or one big difference,' said Gopala, chuckling to himself.

'But, sir, seeing a single mynah is supposed to be unlucky,' said the old man with genuine concern.

Gopala sucked in some air and said, 'Raman, if you see a black cat when you step outside your home, do you turn back? I wouldn't because it is just another being, a creature of God, like the rest of us. I am sure there are good black cats and bad black cats, again like the rest of us. Now, how do you tell apart one cat from the other? Raman, I have already started calling my daughter Mynah. My mother has no opinion on the subject as thankfully she keeps herself aloof from old wives tales. Don't worry, my child will be lucky for herself and for me.'

Raman slunk away at that, stricken at what he rightly assumed was being shown his place.

Gopala had no interest in village life. His father had sent him to a boarding school in Ooty, the hill station that Bangaloreans have traditionally loved for its proximity to their city, the same way Keralites love Bangalore for its proximity to their state.

Cyriac had hoped that Gopala would study well, get a professional degree, then a job overseas and do him proud. But Gopala barely cleared school. His score was so low that Cyriac had to give one lakh rupees in donation, a cultured synonym for bribe, to get him admitted to a decent Bangalore college. Gopala studied arts and majored in philosophy, the only subject he found simple enough to memorise and retain. He graduated with a second class, which by Gopala's academic standards amounted to a distinction.

Gopala was aware that the family had land in the fertile Nilambur that got them decent income but he refused to move back to his ancestral home with its large verandah overlooking jackfruit, mango and papaya trees and delicate banana stalks. The quiet of the place that was broken by susurration of leaves and cooing of birds made him restive. He liked bustle. He would walk down MG Road in Bangalore, where his hostel was located, for coffee. What he liked better was that he could do it without having to stop and smile and talk to every person he passed by, for there was no recognisable face to be spotted. The anonymity energised him.

Cyriac reprimanded himself for keeping his boy away from Nilambur for too long and then sensibly bought land in Jayanagar in Bangalore and built a miniature replica of their home in the city. He sent Shaila to be with their son and visited every weekend, the drive long but pleasurable when he was visiting and depressing on his way back home.

Gopala's friends would land up at the aesthetically put-together home with clean-lined rosewood and rubberwood furniture, and rattan chairs and tables in the veranda outside. They stayed on for lunch and then dinner that Shaila masterfully put together with the cook and the help. She would wait for the boys and the servants to eat first and then serve herself what was left, as a woman of the house ought to. Shaila had mastered this second-hand piety from her parents. She would withdraw into the background unless there were women around, which was not often. When Gopala was with friends, she would pretend to give them space while listening on, fly on the wall, from the other room, to look for lapses in her son's behaviour. She needn't have, for Gopala was a conformist among conformists. When his friends would light up, he would lecture them on the ill-effects of smoking despite the long rounds of ribbing that unfailingly followed. His mother would smile her approval from wherever she was hidden and beam at him later for being so on the straight, so on the narrow.

Chapter 17

'Is she up yet?' Gopala asked Aruna. He was parked at her place for four days now. Aruna shook her head.

'She needs to give her mind some rest,' said Aruna with a reassuring smile.

'It's been almost fourteen hours.'

'She's breathing fine. It will all come rushing back once she's up, that's what she keeps telling us all the time in so many words. We should be happy she is asleep. She is happy for now.'

Gopala looked at the ceiling and sighed. Curtains flew and the antique-finish bronze ceiling fan swayed in its bondage.

'It's quite windy today,' he remarked.

'It's almost monsoon, that's why. But the winds will carry away the clouds. We just need an hour or two of lull for it to rain. It's so humid despite the wind. Should I switch on the AC?'

'I'll do it?' asked Gopala correctly.

She nodded and he did what had to be done before

sitting opposite her on the sofa and asked, 'She met him last year, right? How vain that boy is. Does he have room for anyone else in his life apart from himself? Had they stuck on for one more year she would have bolted for good.'

Both Gopala and Aruna smiled at the thought of a freed Mynah.

Aruna found Gopala's presence comforting. He was among the few men who appeared indifferent to her. Gopala had not allowed himself to seek a woman in flesh since Gracy's leaving to avoid a stepmother situation for his child. He had internalised restraint and forgotten what stirrings felt like outside of visiting certain websites with unfailing regularity. In the past, he never brought home risqué literature for the fear of its discovery by his daughter and mother when she was alive.

Shaila had died in her sleep, a smirk playing non-stop on her dead lips, which a heartbroken Mynah, then thirteen, had kissed while refusing to let go of the body. It had taken Mynah months to be herself again. Gopala was lonelier without his mother, an adult, for company, but never lonely enough to seek a woman.

Aruna looked for chinks and fakeness in his extreme devotion to his child and could find none. She understood his ravaged countenance at the happenings in Mynah's young life. When Aruna had called and told him of the girl's inability to eat or lift herself up for three days, he had insisted that she take her to the best psychiatrist in town immediately.

Mynah had refused to take her father's calls ever since Rohit ghosted her. It cut Gopala to the quick but he was confident that she would come around. He kept calling Aruna instead, who was warned by Mynah to not engage with him for long and not inform him of anything.

Aruna did as told and found the phone number of the famous shrink on the web and dialled him. An hour after their return from his clinic, Gopala landed with a bag filled with clothes and oral rehydration sachets.

Mynah bawled and screamed on seeing him enter the flat. She blamed him for pushing Rohit away and he sank into her bed without a word. When she was depleted, he reached out and cradled her in his arms. Mynah let him without flinching since she had no one else to cradle her.

❦

Though appreciative of it, Aruna was already weary of Gopala's fuss over Mynah and her treatment regime. So she steered the topic towards a neutral direction.

'You run a rubber plantation? Mynah told me.'

'Yes.'

'So what do you do there?'

'It's become a white elephant now that the prices have crashed. The commodity market is at its lowest. None of us are making money. Labour costs are First World and the price of latex, which we tap from the trees and sell, Third World.'

'Why don't you sell the land and reinvest the funds?' asked Aruna, trying to be helpful.

'Perhaps when the cycle turns and demand for natural rubber picks up, someone might offer me a good price for the land. I never thought of selling it before as Nilambur, this place in Kerala where we have this land, is so close to Bangalore. It's just a long drive away, that's all. We had a manager, Raman, who looked after it for decades. Nice man, reliable. After his death, I got a local man, one Kuriakose, to replace him but he has been a pain from day one. I have kept a man to manage the manager. I don't know whether Jacob, the man who mans Kuriakose, is doing his job or has colluded with him while telling me all is okay. But what can I do? Labour is so hard to come by. The workers are mostly from the north and the east of the country, considering locals are not really keen on working on plantations. They are very literate, no? You know that Kerala has hundred per cent literacy. Thank god for other states that don't. Where would we get our workers?'

Aruna laughed and waited for him to continue.

'The work is very intensive. One man must tap around four hundred trees a day.'

'Really? That's a lot.'

'A tapper must start at daybreak. Latex flows much easily

and faster when the temperature is cool. Besides, by noon, it can get really humid and tiring.'

'I know,' said Aruna. 'My husband and I had gone to Kerala for a holiday. It was scorching hot. Only Munnar was cool. It was freezing, in fact. By the way, Kerala was our most expensive trip in the country. Hotel and travel charges were so high in that state, perhaps due to the labour costs.'

'Madam...' began Gopala.

'Oh, please, Gopala, call me Aruna. "Madam" does not make me sound like a decent woman. Though what is decent and what isn't one no longer knows.'

'I'm very sorry, Arunaji.'

'Don't "ji" me either. We must be roughly the same age.'

'Okay, Aruna. I've been wanting to ask you something since the day we first spoke but did not want to sound intrusive. Please don't mind, but when did your husband pass away?'

Aruna laughed.

'He is very much alive and only thing that is "dying" is his hair,' she said, drawing quotation marks in the air. 'He has coloured it dark brown. He left some years ago. He married again.'

'I'm very sorry to hear that,' said Gopala.

Aruna smiled to wipe away the distress that had landed on her guest's face. 'Gopala, I have never been more at peace. That was not the case when he left though. When he walked out, I was frightened like I have never been. I would shiver and roll up in bed like Mynah does now and unlike her I had no one to hold me. My maid would open the door with the spare key she always had. She would bring food from her home and I would barely eat. This went on for a month, by which time my body had almost atrophied. I could barely move my limbs.'

'Did you see a doctor?' asked Gopala, wanting to reach out and take her hand in his.

'No. I woke up one morning, limped to the washroom, got dressed and went out for a walk on the jogging track in the apartment premises. But I felt giddy and returned within five minutes. As days passed, I gradually began to take longer walks. My pace increased. After a week I came back and cooked a proper breakfast and read the papers. Susheela, my maid, was so shocked on seeing me up and about,' said Aruna, laughing.

She continued, 'My brain had to rewire itself to the idea of being single in my middle age. It is scary to grow old alone. But you would know that, Gopala, you've been alone for years.'

'Mynah told you?'

'Yes. Sorry. It's none of my business.'

'No, Aruna. In India everything is everyone's business.'

Gopala chose to open up. It is always easier with strangers.

When his wife left, Gopala recounted, his relatives wanted to know the reason and he did not want to reveal it. He had no clue till date how people found out she had left in the first place and then even the reason so quickly. Some people asked him point-blank for information without hesitating or stuttering.

'It was very difficult. For a long time it seemed impossible to remain sane. I could not imagine how I would have managed to look after Baby if I had a job to go to. I had to pull myself up, feed Baby, put her to sleep and ensure she continued to sleep. You know how kids are. She would cry for hours. Perhaps she sensed the abandonment. To top it, people would come home on the pretext of helping out and try and convince me to remarry.'

There was silence, which Gopala himself broke by saying, 'Her name was Gracy.'

'She was not very gracious,' said Aruna without thinking.

To her shock, Gopala took offence on Gracy's behalf and said, 'Please don't say that. She was forced to marry me. Her parents did not want her to be with her boyfriend who was from a poor family and that too from another religion. Which is why, even though I am not at all happy with the idea of a groom from another region, forget religion, for my daughter, I would not stop her from being happy. Gracy left because leaving felt right to her.'

Aruna felt heat behind her eyelids at the largesse Gopala

was demonstrating towards his runaway wife. She did not doubt the intent of his statement, that it was a kind of bending over backwards to make excuses for Gracy. Aruna's tears came easily, cleansing.

'Aruna, I didn't mean to make you cry. The Gracy chapter was over a long time ago. All parties involved are happy. At least they were till this Rohit fellow came out of nowhere and spoilt it for us,' he said with rising anger.

'Temporarily,' said Aruna, her voice shaky.

'Yes. But right now Baby is deeply unhappy. I agree that she will snap out of it in time. That moron left suddenly, that's all. But I can't watch her suffer.'

Aruna collected herself and said, 'Gopala, everybody gets jilted. Everybody leaves or dies and most of us recover. Scars fade, it is a fact. I can't remember details of Subodh's face when I think of him these days. That is, if I think of him at all, and we were together since we were both nineteen. There is no acrimony. I wish there was. My only complaint is against time lost. Perhaps if I'd borne children it would have been easier. I'll never find out. But if I had taken up a job or a hobby like painting or amateur astronomy, it would have surely helped deal with that sense of bereavement. I was always fascinated by the skies. Dark matter. Gravitational waves. I find the idea of our insignificance in the universe exciting, humbling. But I wasted years, a major portion of a lifetime, with Subodh and on Subodh, and I did not know it. In fact, the other realisation I had was I did not even know him.'

'How so?' asked Gopala, curious to know more about his child's landlord who had become her guardian.

Aruna obliged. 'It was only after he left and I had all the time to myself to analyse and break my head over what went wrong that I realised not being able to father a child killed him. The shortcoming lay on his side, not mine. I did not react to his horror at being told so by a doctor. That was a mistake, yes. He could not process my silent sympathy. He never really touched me after the visit to the doctor, if you know what I mean. I once suggested adoption and that was the only time he screamed at me. He just kept shouting out "no, no, no" and left home without shutting the door. He was a careful man otherwise but that day he did not wait for the elevator. He just ran down. We lived in Prabhadevi then, on the seventh floor of a seven-storey building, a little away from the Siddhivinayak temple.'

She paused and digressed. 'You must visit that temple, Gopala. People walk down to it from all over. They walk for hours to reach it. Most come without any footwear as a form of penance. This happens every Tuesday, Ganesha's day. It is a wish-fulfilment temple. I pleaded with Subodh to visit the temple with me but he flatly refused. I guess on some level I must have felt superior to him as the problem lay with him. These things can get through to the other person even without you yourself knowing it.'

Gopala now rose to Aruna's defence as well—which made her want to laugh.

'But, Aruna, for him to leave you for that is not right. You don't seem to me the kind to leave someone because of a handicap. And even if he had wanted to go, he could have left earlier instead of waiting till you hit your middle age...'

'Do I look old?' interjected Aruna.

'No, of course not. That is not what I meant,' said Gopala, regretting the way he had presented his argument and attempting to made amends.

'Don't get me wrong, but if your husband had moved out earlier, you would have got another shot at a relationship. You do look very good, believe me, and you can get married right now, if you wish. But there is something called the right age. Once it passes, even if the best of a situation presents itself, it cannot bewitch you into accepting it. You are too set in your ways by then. Perhaps that's my Indian mindset speaking.'

'Possibly,' said Aruna, 'but we are talking right now. We are breathing. We are alive. We are enjoying talking to each other. At least, I am. Is there a right age for that? I did not even know you existed till very recently. Yes, I wish I had developed my interest in galaxies far, far away early on. But now that I have been left with a lot of money, I can still pursue what I want. Start from scratch. There are people who learn yoga at eighty, go rappelling from dangerous forts at ninety and even marry at ninety-nine. These are documented cases. I should be able to reclaim my life like these people and I am much younger than them. It's just that I have been paralysed by inactivity for so long. Or maybe I have become plain lazy. What stops anyone with money from doing anything but their own selves?'

'True, true,' said Gopala, assuaging, though he could not see how Aruna was drawing parallels between marriage and hobbies, all the while tying the two with money.

He said thoughtfully, 'You chose to stay true to your husband. Loyalty is not slavery. It is a choice. You kept your interests aside to make him happy. He was your interest, your hobby. You cultivated him. Doing things for someone you love is not waste of a life, Aruna. It is not an investment gone wrong. In the end, the sum total, what counts is how much we give to a passion. It could be anyone or anything. Passion is its own reward: the means and the end.'

Aruna felt tears well up again, at the vouching of her worth, her validation and separation from Subodh at the same time.

'You too can find a woman to spend your old age with,' she let that slide in with a grateful smile that revealed her teeth and inner glow to her audience.

'I am not interested,' said Gopala lightly. 'I am used

to being single and in any case I'd never do anything to jeopardise Mynah's inheritance.'

'You've never had a relationship after Gracy?' asked Aruna, taken aback by the long years of his resolve.

'No.'

'Didn't you want a woman?'

'To be honest, I've always wanted one. But at zero cost. Relationships come with MRP. Too risky.'

Aruna laughed. 'That's true but where has not taking risks got us?'

'Peace and stability also come with MRP. I think their value run into trillions,' said Gopala and looked out of the window.

The breeze had begun to peter out and clouds were able to stay on and gather force. The leaves on the trees that shielded Aruna's flat from the gaze of the neighbouring apartment block had stopped fluttering and tuned into the impending change in weather.

'It will rain in some time,' he said, knowing the behaviour of nature in his farmer blood. 'We shelter parts of rubber trees with plastic covers to keep out rainwater.'

'You were telling me about tapping,' prompted Aruna.

Gopala launched forth: 'A special knife is used to make a cut in the bark of a tree at an angle and a cup placed underneath to collect the latex. It is strung to the bark with a rope to keep it in place. In the olden days the cup was mostly just a half shell of a coconut. Today many use plastic cups. I find these plastic cups ugly but they do last longer than the shells.'

'Does a cup fill up by day end?'

'Much earlier. By late morning. That's when the tapper comes back and pours out the white latex into a bucket. This is apportioned in standard-sized flat basins and mixed with acid and left to coagulate for three to four hours. Then this lump is pressed under a crusher into a thin sheet.

'What do you do with the sheet? Sell it?'

'The sheets are put out to dry. Once dried, they are transferred to what we call a smoke house. They are smoked for two or three days till they turn brown, and then sold.'

'That sounds like a lot of work.'

'Actually, this was how it was done years ago. These days, traders buy the latex directly from us. We sell it by the drum. I was talking of my childhood when we made the sheets ourselves.'

There was a long pause now that the entire procedure of tapping latex from rubber trees had been discussed. Aruna took a romantic mental tour of Kerala during the gap and asked, 'Why did you never settle in your hometown?'

'It is a village, not a town. I find villages deathly boring. Most people do, I guess, otherwise cities would not be getting packed. Now with the internet and the exposure, people want to enjoy the excitement of the big city first-hand. Once you've tasted the stimulation a city offers, village life seems limited and stifling. I was sent to a boarding school in Ooty for my secondary school education. We had students from across the country and some from overseas. Then I went to a college in Bangalore. Villages are great as retreats for those who are stressed or feel they have missed out on a bucolic life that they see as purer or more wholesome and truthful than what cities offer. I think village life is best for an old-age home or those who are comfortable without company, people with an ascetic bent of mind. As a child, I would die to hear the sound of a vehicle whenever I was home for vacations. I'd wait for the roar of any approaching car or an SUV. There are a lot of SUVs in our parts due to the terrain—bumpy roads with sudden bends. I would be so disappointed if it was only my father driving back. Of course, we had no neighbours in the estate. The only time we had some activity was when relatives or my father's friends came visiting. My mother had no friends outside of family and relatives. But things have changed now, more so for women. These days women from our families can be seen driving down to the nearest towns to meet friends for coffee and movies. It's as if the city has come to the village. And yet, people want to shift to the real city.'

He chuckled and said, 'Men settled in villages have such a tough time finding brides. I myself cannot imagine being in a place where I can hear only whooshing of winds and not the din of activity. I want to hear the blaring of cars and screeching of brakes.'

Aruna laughed and said, 'So you were a lonely child, Gopala.'

'Yes, which is why I ensured that Mynah had friends. In the evenings I would take her to the park where I'd be the only father. Not that there were too many mothers around either. Kids Mynah's age were mostly with ayahs.'

He paused and smiled.

'There was this one woman who kept following me. She even asked me out once. Frankly, I was excited but scared and decided not to go back to the park. But then I did not want to keep Mynah from her friends either by cutting short our routine. So I requested a friend of mine to accompany me for a few days and he was kind enough to oblige. The woman was uncomfortable speaking to me in front of him and got the message. When I came alone after some days and did not look at her, she did not pester me again.'

Aruna guffawed. 'What kind of a man are you?'

He looked at her. 'Do you miss a man's company? You don't look like you do. Gracy was my first and only involvement with a woman and it was so shortlived that I never really missed it, except initially when I was dumped. More for Mynah's sake.'

Aruna sobered up and said, 'I don't feel the need for a man now.'

'Was it by mutual consent, the divorce?'

'Yes. No reason asked. The magistrate simply pronounced, "It is done". With these three words, it was officially over. It was a year and a half after we split. We shook hands and he left. I came home and watched TV. By then I'd already got my first paying guest. You know, that was the first time I made my own money after so many years. Even if it was just rent earned from Subodh's parting gift. This flat.'

'Don't you miss him? I mean, after all this time together? I still miss Gracy, though I spent barely any with her.'

'This may sound odd to you but if he'd left soon after we had got together, I would have been completely broken. But being with a person for this long reduces them to routine. You've seen them groggy with sleep, pick their nose or fart after coming home from a party in a celebrity home. But it's not that I did not miss him. Initially, I missed the farts too,' said Aruna, laughing. 'But it was a dull ache. Actually, I don't know whether I am making sense. I now believe that I never really knew him as initially I was madly in love with him and later I had no real interest in knowing what he was thinking. We had been together for so long that I did not feel the urge to reach out and find out what was going on inside his head. We were never really partners. I was the so-called trophy wife, to be polished and shown off. Every time someone said I looked good, he'd gloat. That changed after the doctor's verdict about his sperm count. He was deeply unhappy and punished me by forgetting me. I am sure he is still unhappy and that he does not know how to be at peace, though he pretends to be so with Harsha. That's his wife.'

'You've met her?'

'She ensured that. He walked out of this flat with her. Both had come home to pack his stuff.'

'She literally stole him from you after all these years?'

Aruna smiled. 'Subodh was not mine to lose. No one can snatch anyone unless they are up for the snatching. I only missed the habit.'

Aruna switched off the AC and opened the window, but the air outside was heavy and still. As she turned towards the room, she caught Gopala's eyes and for a split second thought she was looking at Mynah. She smiled more warmly than she would have otherwise and began to speak with a familiarity that Gopala was trained not to react to.

'You are not over Gracy yet, Gopala. Otherwise you would have at least had a fling,' she picked up the thread.

'I'm not. But even if I were, remarriage would not have been an option.'

'How was she?'

'She was lovely. She laughed a lot like Baby, like Mynah.'

'Please call her Baby. It suits her. Let's check on her.'

'Yes, let's wake her up so that she can go back to missing that idiot.'

Chapter 18

Rohit was on site. He was to execute a design for an office layout in a large commercial complex at Andheri, a crowded western suburb where the headquarters of a few large companies had shifted and many fledgling start-ups had set up shop for the connectivity offered by the metro.

The lawn was to be hedged and partitioned with topiaries. The borders were to be beautified further with foxtail ferns and fishtail plants and the turf was to be carpeted with American bluegrass. He was informing the contractor about the two trucks needed to transfer soil and fertilisers to fill the space when his phone rang. He excused himself and stepped a little away.

'Hey,' he said, smiling.

'Hey,' said Mynah.

'Do you miss me?' asked Rohit.

'I'm missing myself.'

'I'll just wind up and come. Put on that top we bought yesterday.'

'I'm already wearing it.'

Rohit fidgeted and said he would call her back. He walked back to the team, said his grandmother was dead and feverishly walked to his car.

'He was so passionate about me, doctor. Once he left an important site at Andheri, which is so far from our place, to meet me using his grandmother's death as an excuse. I would never do that and told him so. He got mad at that, but later he was so sweet and apologised so many times. One evening, he stood outside my office totally drenched in rain only to make sure I got a cab. You know how difficult it is to get one when it pours. I don't know where the drivers disappear. I know Rohit loves me. Love cannot be switched off like a button. But he has decided to stay away and pretends to be not interested.'

Gopala who had tagged along with Mynah felt like shaking her till she saw sense. Dr Radhakrishnan noticed Gopala's irritation and asked him to wait outside. The doctor kept silent till the door shut and turned towards his young patient whose cheeks had got some colour now and eyes sparkle. He could take risks.

'Mynah, when a man acts this passionate about a woman, he is acting out his desire for passion itself. The woman may be x, y or z. It does not matter. It is a non-issue. Any man who can get so involved with a woman overnight that it seems like madness can completely disengage overnight too because this kind of baseless passion can tire anyone out. Do you get me, child?'

'But love cannot be extinguished overnight,' Mynah said with authority.

'So maybe it wasn't overnight. See, Mynah, there are people who love the idea of love, but can sustain it for only that long. They then find another object to shower their affection on. I'm not saying Rohit has found anyone else. I am sure he has not. But from what you tell me there was no friendship in your equation. Don't feel bad, ma. He stood under your apartment wing and sought you out. He waited for you outside your office because he liked your face. But there was no real foundation to your relationship. You are so pretty and intelligent. Any man would fall for you. Rohit is no different. He will regret his mistake at some point. Very soon, I am sure of it.'

Mynah smiled broadly at the compliment and then remembered to resume whining. 'But he was my first and only love, doctor. And are you sure he has not found anyone else?'

'He told me he hasn't and I can spot a lie.'

'Thank god.'

'Mynah, what I am trying to say here is that it does not matter even if he has. Forget him. For a moment imagine you have hurt your head in an accident. If the man cared for you, he would have dropped everything and run to you. The same way he stood outside your building and office and I don't know how many places he found to stand.'

Mynah laughed bitterly at that. Dr Radhakrishnan was encouraged to speak further by the laughter, though unpleasant.

'I told him that you had been brought in to see me and that you were not in a good shape. He could have come from wherever he was to you, to make it better. That's what we would do even for a regular friend.'

Mynah looked down and sat still, processing what was said. A very faint Hindustani classical recital by Bhimsen Joshi filled the room, its phantom sound nudging Mynah into asking the doctor whether it was playing at all. The doctor looked around, denied knowledge of any music in his clinic and then winked at her. Mynah nodded, got up and left without sound.

The doctor's work was done. The recovery would hasten itself.

⚶

After a quiet ride back to the flat, Gopala left for the airport to fetch Ramya the cook whom he had booked into a flight. Driver Mani, her husband, was on his way from Bengaluru to Mumbai in Gopala's car, a distance of close to a thousand kilometres. Gopala wanted to recreate the home Baby had flown from, like his father had done for him. Ramya and Mani were to share a flat he had rented in a redeveloped building nearby.

Gopala looked sideways at Aruna as the elevator door opened. She waved. In response, he showed her an open palm, with its straight and curved lines and grooves, before disappearing from her sight.

Chapter 19

A CARPET OF GOLDEN COPPER POD AND RUSTY GULMOHAR flowers was being swept by large garden brooms, unmindful of the fresh shower of petals that mockingly undid their job immediately. Each tree was blessed with countless blossoms in hot and rainy months.

As Mynah was walking under the trees that lined the compound of Jamuna Heights, lightly squishing the patchy yellow and red floral carpet with her strident shoes, a pigeon dropping landed on her purple dress.

Mynah stopped and smirked as a bit of the goo caught on to her fingers when she ran a hand over the targeted sleeve. She wiped it off with a tissue as she did not want to be late for work.

'That's too bad. On your way out,' said Rohit, appearing out of nowhere.

Mynah squinted as a fiery sun found its way through an opening in a tree and interrupted her vision.

'Oh, hello there. Forget it. Bird shit is supposed to be lucky, especially if it lands on your head. Then it's a real blessing.'

Rohit laughed at the easy opening.

'I'm Rohit, by the way. I came to your place the other day. You had dropped a book in the elevator.'

'So, you were the Romeo? I guessed so. I'm very sorry to not have returned your book. I'd started out the same day but got a phone call and forgot about it,' she said.

He moved his eyes downward.

'Okay. Confession,' he capitulated. 'I did make up the dropped book excuse. My imagination is limited that way. I'm a landscape architect. I can only think of visual, tactile excuses to get through to pretty girls.'

'Clearly,' she said.

He was lost as she looked at him patiently, waiting to move on. All she wanted to tell him was that he was the pretty one between the two, and that she had a lot lined up at work.

'Okay then. See you,' he said dejectedly, not wanting to end the short interaction.

'Bye, bye,' she replied, obviously relieved at being let off.

He watched her walk away and measured the distance till his mental tape ran out.

Shaila was drawing kohl whorls on her grandchild's forehead and cheeks to ward off the evil eye. Mynah was cooing up to her from the cloth hammock strung to an iron hook on the ceiling that swung at touch. Gopala was lying on his low, rectangular four-poster bed next to the hammock, his eyes fixed on the ceiling. He felt no ache following the abrupt disappearance of his wife as he had been given an anti-anxiety pill by the family doctor. Despite his blunted senses, he jumped out of bed when Mynah began to whimper. Shaila smiled at him and watched her son reach out for Baby. She did not feel his muted pain. Mynah had inherited some of Shaila's indifference. She felt her own pain keenly though.

Rohit counted hours till she would enter the lobby again and glide into his reality. He had taken a week off from work for the purpose.

Mynah got a text from Rohit.

'Call if awake.'

She pressed the call button. He picked up at first ring.

'Hey,' he said.

'Hey.'

'How are you?' he asked.

'I'm good,' said Mynah mechanically, her voice a whisper.

'Would you have my hairclip-shaped pen drive? It's got some of my office files on it.'

Mynah felt a sob escape her.

'It's in my bag,' she got the words out.

'Oh, thank god. I'll collect it after work,' he replied, ignoring the break in her voice.

Niceties were out of the way and the call was cut short.

Mynah sobbed. Aruna hugged her. She struggled out of the clasp and ran towards Gopala.

When she was five, Vedant had broken Moltu, her talking boy doll with blue eyes that shut and opened when he spoke till his battery-operated machine died. He had stopped moving his eyes ages ago but spoke to Mynah when no one was around.

'Baby, why was grandma upset with you?' Moltu asked.

'She is always after me to eat. She found me under the bed and dragged me to the table and gave me a mountain of beans. I ate a hundred kilos of beans.'

'A hundred kilos! How did it all fit inside your stomach?'

'I packed some in my stomach and then I went to the toilet and threw it out of my bum and made space for more,' said Mynah with much importance.

'You are so smart, Baby. You are the smartest person in the world. You are a thousand hundred times smarter than Suby, Vedant, Mythili and Rinki,' said Moltu with open admiration.

Mynah went up to Vedant when he came home to play and

told him what Moltu thought of her. Vedant began to shiver with rage, his face reddened and eyes shrank and began to water. He ran to her toy box, dragged out Moltu and punched him till he bled and lay unconscious. Mynah screamed for help but before grandma and Suzy aunty, Vedant's mother, could find them, Moltu's body and clothes lay in tatters.

'I'm very sorry for what I did to Moltu, Mynah,' said Vedant with genuine feeling.

'It's alright, Vedant, we were kids then,' she replied mechanically.

Vedant was visiting Mynah during his winter break from Columbia University in New York. They were both adults now. Politeness is popular among their kind.

'My mom told me about the murder today. Frankly, I have no recollection of it. I must have been really mad that Moltu found you so smart. I still want to be the smartest,' said Vedant, trying to make her laugh.

'Yes, you are the smartest. Now that you know you are very smart, you are no longer mad at him, right?' she asked with forced equanimity.

Vedant smiled tightly and said, 'In any case, I wanted to say sorry for breaking your favourite toy. You must have loved it a lot.'

Mynah got up and went to her room. She found Moltu's

naked arms, legs, head and torso and torn shirt folded neatly beside him in the toy box; an ayah had lost his trousers during an annual cleaning. She gathered Moltu's parts and shirt and went out. Vedant looked on horrified and said, 'He looks like Chucky, that scary doll from *Child's Play*. I'm so, so sorry.'

'I still love him, Vedant. He was my first friend. We used to have long conversations.'

'Like Calvin and his toy tiger.'

'We are both single children so we decided to adopt each other as brother and sister.'

'He must have been a very odd brother to tell his sister that she was a million times smarter than him. Hasn't he heard of sibling rivalry?'

Both laughed and the tension eased. Vedant picked up Moltu and offered to get new clothes stitched for him. Mynah told him to let it be.

'This is his second life. He is damaged but he is still alive and I love him the way he is.'

'Mynah, you loyalist. But I'm finding you a bit scary, dude.'

Mynah laughed.

'We are a part of the *Child's Play* franchise, remember? We are ze zombies.'

The two were childhood friends and there was no requirement for veiled parrying or making up. They went out for coffee with Mythili, their only other friend who was still in Bangalore. The rest had left for elsewhere for higher studies. Mynah would leave in a year.

Rohit came to her room, looked and looked away. He took his pen drive from Mynah, carefully ensuring not to touch her fingers, thanked the curtains and left.

Chapter 20

'HEY, WE MEET AGAIN,' HE SAID.

'Were you waiting for me?' Mynah asked good-naturedly.

'Yes. Want to meet me for lunch during your break at work?' he got out the question nervously.

'I am sorry,' she said, weightily. 'I have a con-call lined up at work today. I'm a copywriter so I have to be responsible.'

A hurting Rohit watched Mynah get into a cab.

She reached her glass and wood office on the thirty-second floor of a building in a rehabilitated mill complex. She loved the office and its aerial view.

Not too many people were around yet. She switched on her workstation and browsed the web next to Varun, a senior copywriter who was watching an animation film on his terminal. He had cheered up further on spotting her.

'Happy? Now I'll do what makes me happy. You should have seen my dad's face when I said that after handing over my engineering degree to him and then told him that I

still wanted to join advertising. He looked like I'd asked for his liver. In any case it is one organ that supposedly grows back,' Varun had told Mynah on their first meeting to make her laugh.

Mynah had doubled up on cue and Varun had snatched a glance at her even teeth and amber eyes. Her lips would tilt down when she'd begin to smile and then edge upwards in what came as a surprise. Her head was a bounce of curls, which she kept medium-short, above her shoulders, and her firm body appeared to be perpetually in motion.

Pad was already seated at the table next to the phone with his team of seven. Varun tugged Mynah's t-shirt and prodded her to make her point with his eyes.

She launched forth, 'For this TV spot, I was thinking of a hero type of a guy, a typical Mumbai dude. A goon who leches at girls and passes cheap remarks, which we will beep out, of course. And this young girl, a plus-two student, who is waiting for a bus outside her school in her uniform with a haversack on her back, takes out her water bottle and sprays it on his face. Soon, the other girls around do the same and it begins to rain, as if the gods are with them. They then heroically tear open the gum pack with their teeth and turn to enter a bus that pulls in, in slow-mo. We will end with the tag line, "iss gum mein hai kitna dum" in

Hindi and "chew bang!" in English. In fact, "chew bang!" can play on a loop in the background like an anthem when these girls are walking towards the bus.'

Pankaj, the visualiser, patted her. Pad gave her a thumbs-up.

'Now, why do I get that been there, done that feel?' Mangs' voice drawled out of the phone. He was seated in his office in Delhi.

Mangesh was the marketing man of the multinational client company, a fast-moving consumer goods giant that had hired Ad Grande for a three-sixty-degree campaign for its bubble gum brand—from print to electronic media to online. If her idea were to be accepted, Mynah would be in a respectable league in her agency. Two of her earlier ideas had been partially executed, one for Rajasthan tourism where she had presented a concept of camels wearing colourful turbans and walking right through various monuments in different zones of changing topography. At the end, a camel smiles into the camera and says, 'ghani khamma'—'hello' in Marwari—though the phrase's literal translation would be 'we seek your forgiveness; a lot of it'. Mynah had done weeks of research for the ad. By the end of the campaign, the south Indian girl could speak the two Marwari words like a local, right down to the accent. The line was accepted though the turbans were not.

This had been the high point of her young career, and

won her team an award. She wore a saree for the function and was kissed by all in her team, except Varun who kept looking around as if he had lost something.

The other campaign was for an ambitious, unknown brand of umbrellas from the north-eastern state of Assam that wished to go national. She had insisted on not showing any rain. She wanted the umbrella to be carried for lunches and dinners, like an accessory, instead of a clutch. All the umbrellas in the ad should be colourful and feminine but for one, she had suggested. At the end, a man would open the most expensive umbrella of the brand, of the long raven-black grandfather variety with a curved wooden stick, and hold out an arm for his girlfriend. They would walk under a scorching sun. The tagline was: 'Hey, what umbrella are you wearing today?' This idea got her a standing ovation from her team, though the client was not comfortable with sunshine all the time and insisted on heavy rain for the last shot to showcase the product's real utility. Her confidence shot up and she felt blessed to have entered the profession.

Mynah smiled through the rest of the three-hour-long client con-call with Mangs and excused herself from the usual team lunch after a marathon session. Varun was overtly concerned when she spoke of both a headache and a stomach ache before heading towards the washroom. Pad touched her forehead and did not speak. He knew heartbreak needed a toilet seat to play first-stage counsellor.

She left the washroom after flushing away some of her disappointment in what she had thought would be her big break with a big multinational. Pad, Varun and Crystal, her friend from the client-servicing department, had promised her idea would be a sure-shot hit, that it would sail through and bring her to the next level in her career. She had gone to the meeting nervous with anticipation, but sure of herself.

She slunk out of the washroom and the office, her tote heavy on her shoulder.

⚜

She stepped out of the cab, forgetting to thank the driver, and entered her complex gate when she noticed Rohit.

'Hey. Want to grab a coffee?' he asked.

Mynah shrugged an 'alright' because she did not know what to do with the rest of the evening or even her life for that matter and wished to postpone sharing the news of her rejection with Aruna.

They walked out of the complex that exited into a lane so narrow that if two cars were to come face to face, one would have to reverse to allow the other to pass. Large trees lined a garden to the left of the lane and the chawl marked its other boundary.

It was July and two weeks since Rohit had seen her. The

air was humid and tiring as it had not rained for days. The government was discussing water cuts to tide over what the weather department had them believe would be a mostly dry monsoon. Farmers in the parched parts of Maharashtra were killing themselves over multiplying debts with no hope of repayment as the sowing season had not been followed by rainfall yet again. City denizens did read and watch news about farmers and see images of their lined foreheads and unsmiling faces next to dried up farms and dying cattle. But they quickly flipped the pages of newspapers, switched television channels and scrolled down their hand-held devices and forgot about the devastation as farms to them were fun weekend destinations. They did not see the undeniable link between those who tilled the land and the food placed on attractive supermarket shelves. They irritably thought of the rationing of water as having to hit the shower earlier in the day before taps ran dry, and casually hoped it would rain, though not after they left home in shiny outfits.

It should only rain over lakes or touristy spots, Rohit would tell his friends who'd agree and describe an overcast sky as drab and dull. But Mynah looked forward to monsoon and the fresh fragrance of the earth upon its mating with the first rain. She was after all an expat farmer's daughter, though the farmers of Kerala led a very different existence from their counterparts in Maharashtra where she lived now. It rained often and in plentiful in Nilambur. She loved

Nilambur. From a distance, it is easy to long for closeness.

꧁ꕥ꧂

Mynah walked on, her head tilted and eyes listless. Rohit, who had made it his mission to impress her, pointed to the trees and said, 'I wish there were more aromatic trees in this area. I know it is fanciful thinking but I wish there were a few eucalyptus trees on one side for their minty scent and a line of perennial flowering plants like milkweed and oleander on the other for their beauty. Between the trees there could be little perfumed shrubs of jasmine, gardenia and murraya exotica. This walk would have been far more interesting with these around, don't you agree?'

'I like our gulmohars,' said Mynah distractedly, her self-indulgent thoughts on the tragedy at work.

'Gulmohars flower during summer,' enthused Rohit. 'It's July and they are mostly gone. We need a lot more natural colour around us. At least rain-trees and mehendi look radiant in their luxurious foliage and branches. Like this one above us. They make up for a lack of flowers by nesting chirpy sunbirds, parakeets and sparrows that are nature's Bach and Mozart. Look, there's one sparrow right there.'

Mynah looked up and met Rohit's eyes on the way down. He felt faint.

'Rohit, what is the point that you making here? It's only a little sparrow. Do you always talk shop? You must care a lot about your work.'

This was not the reaction Rohit had expected.

'I'm so sorry to have bored you, Mynah. I guess I was trying to make you think of me as a great romantic character. Not someone who works with his sleeves and trousers rolled up planting trees in clay loam all day.'

Mynah laughed. 'What's clay loam?'

'It's a mixture of sand, silt and clay that is used to father a robust garden.'

'We call it mud. Plain mud. My father spends a lot of time with his sleeves rolled up in our garden back home in Bangalore. So I don't find the idea of anyone even rolling their entire body in mud odd. You can roll in mud as much and for as long as you wish. My blessings and my father's blessings are always with you, child.'

They walked down a kilometre to reach the coffee shop filled with mostly single people peering into their laptops. There were also a few couples in various stages of coupling. The newer ones were all hands and eyes, the older ones sat a little apart, each their own person again. One pair was business-like and transactional, the two gauging each other, perhaps for an arranged marriage or a job. Their vibe was pleasant and uncluttered by emotion.

'I still can't believe you agreed to come out with me,' said Rohit, pulling out a chair for Mynah.

Mynah ignored the effusiveness and said, 'So, tell me,

Rohit. Why is it so important for you to hang out with me? Are you from Mumbai or from elsewhere like me?'

'I'm very much from here.'

'You must have had friends here all your life. You have a job. You are not ugly and yet you end up waiting for me.'

'I find you beautiful,' he said sincerely.

Mynah laughed at that and slapped his thigh.

'It's not funny, Mynah,' Rohit sounded crushed. 'Mynah, Mynah. What a name. Mynah. I have been thinking of you a lot since that day in the lift.'

'Aruna aunty told me that you were into me but now I can see that for myself, dude,' she rolled her eyes and demonstrated her lopsided grin. As she leaned forward to sip her affogato, her elbow brushed against his. He felt faint again. They were at the kindergarten stage of a relationship.

'Tell me, Mynah. Be frank. Don't you find me attractive?' he asked desperately.

Mynah roared inside the already noisy coffee shop, her laughter echoing off the walls, and said, 'Let me look. Okay... so you have brown eyes, a sharp nose and nice lips. A good crop of brownish hair. You could pass off as a Turkish fellow. Are you?'

'I'm Guj.'

'Listen, Rohit from Gujarat, I have never dated anyone and no one so far has ever asked me out.'

'I don't believe you,' he said, genuinely shocked.

'You should. Why would I lie? My dad always timed my movements. Not that I mind. He's the best father ever. So I was either going to school or coming back from school or going to college or coming back from college. I had loads of friends back home in Bangalore and on some weekends I would go out with them in our car or someone else's for movies and grub and come back home by car, blah blah blah... We have a farm estate in Kerala. Bangalore is a long drive from the estate. We would visit it together some weekends. We would go on trips all over the place every vacation. My mother left us when I was a baby. So my dad doubled up as two parents. I had a grandmother though, who was equally angel-like. My dad would never leave me home alone with her too, unless it was an emergency and that has happened only twice. Once when our manager had a heart attack and he had to rush to Nilambur to sort out his medical insurance, and the other time over some labour issue. Both times he was back in a day. Constant parental supervision apart, I've been too busy studying and now working hard to really notice attractive boys.'

'What manager?'

'Of our estate.'

'Don't you think it's a bit odd that you have never felt the need to date?' he asked, steering off the inconsequential.

'No,' she said and took a sip of her hot-cold dessert drink.

'Have you ever crushed on anyone?' he asked.

'Yes, Justin Timberlake and Justin Bieber: one stud-like, the other a pretty boy like yourself.'

'Quite an eclectic taste I must say, Lady Mynah. But anyone real? Flesh and blood?'

'No.'

'You've never felt any... needs?'

'No,' said Mynah and gave him a naughty smile.

Rohit frowned. 'And no one's asked you out?'

'No. Is it such a big deal? I mean, I used to go out with my friends and now with my colleagues who are my friends for lunches and Aruna aunty whom you met the other day, but no one has been in love with me or I with them.'

'People must be besotted with you and you must not have noticed. Did you notice that I was?'

'Aruna aunty told me and now you yourself have.'

'Have you explored Tinder? It's so much fun. A hook-up always does one good. Swipe right and daddy wouldn't know. You could have a fling. You could have a fling with me.'

'Yeah, yeah, I know. I know. I'm not a baby. By the way, that's my pet name. Baby. But why are you obsessing over my non-existent love life? You think it is abnormal to not have one? Okay, let's go back. Aunty will be waiting,' said Mynah abruptly, retrieving her tote hanging off the chair.

'How are you two related?'

'We are not. I live with her as a paying guest. She takes good care of me. Okay, now let's split the bill. I cannot let you fund my drink and sandwich. Are you vegetarian, being a Gujarati?'

'No. I first experimented with non-vegetarian food with my former girlfriend.'

He waited for a jealous reaction but Mynah looked at him in anticipation of what he would say next.

'We broke up since we wanted different things from life,' he said, deflated that she had not pursued the subject.

'Is wanting different things bad?' she asked soberly, pushing back thoughts which if revealed would dim the lights of the coffee shop.

'There is an optimal level of different things that partners can afford to want. A relationship is like an elastic band. You head off in opposite directions and at some point the bond snaps.'

'So wise you sound. At what point exactly does a band snap?' she asked and waited for a break in the conversation to leave the cafe.

'If both always want to do something other than what the other person wants, it can get boring,' he said, lying glibly. They had wanted very similar things.

'Possibly. That sounds like a cool reason to get up and leave. All for the best, right? Let's go?' she asked.

Rohit did not show any sign of vacating his chair. He

looked respectfully at Mynah and said, 'You are different from the other girls I've met.'

'Haven't you heard? Every human being is different like everybody else? This is the lamest pickup line, bro,' Mynah said.

'Don't bro me. For someone who's never been picked up, you sure know a lot,' he teased her.

'I read. I YouTube. What's so extraordinary about knowing basic stuff?'

'You still haven't answered my question. Do you think I'm attractive?'

'More attractive than me.'

Mynah walked back with Rohit in the first flush of a freshly forged tie, the way it happens on the slopes and climbs of the rolling tea gardens of Munnar that made up some of her happiest childhood memories. She was back amongst the protective trees that gift timelessness to the hills. It was as if a billion blue Neelakurinji flowers had bloomed in the high ranges after generations. It felt like coming home.

Chapter 21

Mynah was lying on Gopala's lap in her room and he was stroking her curls. Aruna walked in with a bowl of rustic vegetable, rice and lentil soup.

'Doesn't it smell good, Baby?' he asked while mouthing a 'thank you' to Aruna who hovered around.

'What?'

'Your soup's here. Full of minerals and vitamins and protein and carbohydrates and...'

Mynah smiled. When she was little, her daddy would end the lyrical breaking down of nutrients by tickling her senseless. He would then mock-blow into the soup spoon to cool the already lukewarm concoction, always the same comforting, fragrant mix. She would mock-blow into the air with him, in tandem, till her father would stop, and slurp it down imperially as a reward for his buffoonery, ingrate as children are to parents' untiring attempts to feed them and watch them grow into robust adults.

She turned to Gopala and asked, 'Daddy, why do you really think mummy left? I would have never gone anywhere if I were with you.'

A four-year-old Mynah had first asked about Gracy when Gopala had gone to pick her up at her kindergarten class. Her face was lined with grey dried-up rivulets. She had never known her mother except instinctively to suckle. Most children in her class were dropped and picked up by theirs and Mynah wanted hers to do likewise.

'She's gone where she is very happy,' Gopala had said.

'Does she have babies?'

'No. I don't think she is capable of looking after babies. She was herself like a baby, that's why she left.'

'She could have played with me and Moltu. I play with big people like you. Mummy is not nice.'

'No, Baby. She is very nice. She loves you. She cannot come back since she lives very far from our house, otherwise she would have rushed back in a flash.'

The response had brought an uncertain smile to her face.

When she was a little older, he decided to be more specific and truthful.

'If she didn't love you, she would not have called me before leaving. She would have just left. She did not want you to cry. When I reached home you were asleep.'

Over the years, the questions got nuanced and textured, but her tone was always curious, never grudging, due to Gopala's presentation of Gracy's leaving and Mynah's trust in her father.

❦

She turned to sit up, taking off Gopala's hand from her head and asked, 'Did she ever stroke my head like you do?'

'Yes, I remember she did.'

'What was her boyfriend's name again?'

Gopala answered from the distance of two decades.

'Hemanth.'

'Not a happening name, no?'

Gopala laughed, heartened by her repartee.

'Why were you named Gopala, Daddy? It's as unusual a name as mine in our families. I never got down to asking earlier.'

'Baby, children are rarely interested in their parents' history unless it concerns them. My parents were childless for years. Then my father met a face reader at a tea shop on his way to Ramapuram where he had taken a short halt. The man took one look at him, patted his shoulder and said things would be fine.'

'Things would be fine,' Mynah repeated. 'What does that mean?'

'He told my father I know you are suffering but this suffering is for your spiritual growth. It is your karmic journey. You are paying back your karmic debts or something like that.'

'So? What does that have to do with your name?' asked Mynah, demonstrating her exasperation.

'His name was Gopala,' said Gopala and smiled.

'Your father was so impressed by the man and his speech that he named his only child after him?'

'He was a face reader, Baby. There are people like that who take one look at you and know what is going on in your mind. They can tell you on what date you will do what and how. They can see things before they happen. They can travel back and forth in time.'

'In their mental time machine? You believe all this nonsense, Daddy?'

'I don't know. I believe in the power of the mind, its potential,' said Gopala tapping his right temple.

'Like Sherlock's mind palace. You are so superstitious, Daddy,' Mynah did an eyeroll, her most common expression when with Gopala and Rohit.

Gopala continued, 'He told my father that six years hence he would be blessed with a son who would be like an angel and he would be everything that one ever wishes for in a child. That his wait would be worth it. I don't know about the angel bit. Maybe my father made it up to please me. I was so bad at studies and didn't do anything other than manage the estate, which in any case is being managed by a manager. I'm just a figurehead. I've not added to our property. I've simply floated on, like a kite on the loose.'

'But you are an angel,' cried Mynah. 'You have led such

a super-duper decent life. Have you ever cheated anyone? Never.'

'Baby, according to you, anybody who leads a boring predictable life is an angel.'

'Yes. You are my boring angelic father. We will rename you Angel. Have you never felt like remarrying? For yourself? I know you have told me many times that you did not marry again for me. It's such a huge sacrifice. I am sure you would have been second-time lucky. You can still do it.'

'First of all, your mother never asked me for a divorce. She just lived in with Hemanth and then moved in with his brother as I have told you. I don't know his name. She must have had her reasons for moving on. I don't know why she never asked for a divorce. If she has remarried, I will not file a case against her for bigamy or anything like that. As far as my not remarrying is concerned, I can safely say that I did not marry for myself. It made me happy to see you happy. So, I did what made me happy. There is no sacrifice in doing what one wants to do for oneself. I didn't want to risk what I had for what I didn't only to experience so-called conjugal bliss. I did not want a stepmother for you. People can behave in strange ways, Mynah. Their ambitions and desires can make them do unpleasant things and I am not willing to pay the price of peace for something as trivial as companionship.'

Mynah pulled Gopala towards her with her young arms

and kissed him on a cheek and asked, 'What was so special about that Hemanth? I should not say this but Mummy sounds a little less smart.'

'You should never say such things, Baby, and that too about your own mother.'

'But she did leave us for him. You had told me that he was very handsome.'

'I've never seen him but that's what I had heard. She was young, Baby. Roughly your age. She would not have known of things like consequences. There are people who go through their entire lives not thinking of them. Sometimes I think it is wiser not to be extra-wise and let repercussions take care of themselves. People who live for the moment, I feel, might be way smarter than most of us who are worriers.'

'How old was she when she left?'

'Twenty-four.'

Mynah sat up in bed, her eyes more alive than they had been of late. 'I want to meet her.'

Gopala had evaded this inevitability. This time he had to look it in the eye. There was no way round it.

He went to meet Dr Radhakrishnan who gave his blessings for the meeting, saying a visit from her absconding mother might prove cathartic. In any case, it was more than four weeks since Rohit had disappeared so she was in safe territory, he said.

'The reunion will be safe, I promise,' he had said across

the table that separated him from those who approached him for a shot at balance.

Gopala went up to Mynah and said unevenly, 'I'll visit her in Bangalore and request her to come here to see you. I've got her address from her uncle. He sounded so happy to hear my voice and believes that a rapprochement is in the offing. People presume so much.'

'Oh, stop blabbering, Daddy. Go now. Leave.'

Gopala wore his shoes, took his wallet, waved at Mynah and Aruna, and left for the airport.

Chapter 22

Mᴙɴᴀʜ WALKED UP TO THE BASIN IN HER BATHROOM and washed her face. She looked at her reflection in the rectangular mirror stuck against the wall, its muted golden frame speckled with miniature parrots. The birds were not caged and yet destined to be trapped inside the frame: inanimate, two-dimensional and incomplete.

Am I looking at myself or a mishmash of chance DNA that created me? Am I anything more than a mere accident in a loveless marriage?

Mynah thought these thoughts as she held on to the basin with one hand and wiped her eyes with the back of the other.

She went to the living room and saw Gopala lying on the slate-grey divan. Aruna had pulled up a chair from the dining table and was pressing her father's head. The room smelled of balm.

'What a role reversal, Daddy,' she remarked.

'Baby, your Aruna aunty is spoiling me. She is too good with her hands,' he said and the pressure on his forehead increased in acknowledgement.

'How is Daddy?' Mynah whispered as Aruna gingerly got up and spread a quilt over him.

'He needed to meet her more than you did.'

Gopala had thought he would collapse while lifting his finger to ring the doorbell, the beat in his chest so hard that it threatened to pulp him comatose.

The door was opened by an ancient man, his face shrivelled by poverty and a lifetime of slavery, his world view limited to his employer's home and needs.

'Yes, sir?' he asked, the upper half of his body permanently bent.

'Is madam home?' asked Gopala, his voice a squeak.

'Yes, she is. Are you Gopala sir? I will call her,' said the man ushering him in.

Gopala did as told and waited, clearing his throat multiple times.

The curtain that separated the drawing room from the rest of the flat was drawn back and Gracy appeared. Gopala looked up and knew he had chased a ghost for two decades.

She ran towards him and hugged him for long-lasting seconds, pulling away to look at him with a coquettish smile that made Gopala step back. An open hug was not what he had expected. He had imagined shaking hands with her at best, not the guiltless bonhomie the hug conveyed.

'So, Gopala, you finally came looking for me,' she said revealing her teeth that had survived ageing. Her pearlies had managed to implant themselves in Mynah's mouth as well.

'Mynah wants to meet you,' he said after clearing his throat yet again.

'Oh, how is she?' Gracy asked with much interest.

'She had a breakdown after her boyfriend broke off with her,' said Gopala.

She threw a hand backwards and said, 'Tell her she will be okay.'

Gopala lidded his rage at the indifferent response and said, 'I've come to request you to accompany me to Bombay. She's there right now. She found a job and that moron in that city. She's not in the position to travel.'

A look of discomfort flitted across Gracy's face. 'Is she in such a bad state that she cannot come down to Bangalore? There are so many good doctors here.'

'She can't travel. Not at this point, no. She wants to meet you. Her doctor, a psychiatrist, and he's supposed to be good, has agreed to allow you to visit her and in fact said it would help her. She's feeling abandoned right now and wants to fix at least one relationship.'

'So you think I abandoned her?' Gracy muttered in self-righteous anger.

Gopala sighed, sat down and unspooled: 'Look, Gracy. I have never used your leaving to turn Mynah against you. At the same time, I did not ever tell her that her mother was dead or concoct a lie. I have always put facts before her and she has understood as best as a child can. She wants closure. All I can offer her is a chance to tie up at least one loose end by ensuring you'll meet. Please come. Be with her for an hour or two. It will make her feel better. That boy is a snake and I am glad he has slithered away. He is not from our community. Not that I have any issues with community or caste or region or even nation, especially since you were coerced into marrying me against your wishes. Even so, I'll be honest. I will be happier if she finds someone from among our own people. I would feel safer that way, although we both know it is not an insurance against anything in life.'

Gopala knew he was contradicting himself. Worried about ticking off Gracy, he took a mental step back and said, 'I think that boy was simply looking for an excuse to run. He seems the type. I cannot bear to see Mynah go about her days mechanically. She's been this way for about a month. There has been some improvement with all the medication but it's only slight. She sleeps like a... She's been prescribed such heavy medication. Baby was always a healthy, happy child. That loser has brought her to this. I did not even know so many medicines existed.'

He heaved and Gracy's eyes moistened at the scene

playing out, as if in a movie. It was so removed from her life. She did not know these people.

She went to her room and called up Kalyan, Hemanth's brother, and told him she was leaving for Bombay to see her daughter who was very ill. Her former husband was here to take her. She sounded like a martyr to Kalyan's love-struck ears. He asked her to take care and not load too much stress on herself. She sighed into the phone and after disconnecting went in to change.

What do I wear? A saree will look too old-fashioned. It has to be a salwar kameez. I'll put on the new bottle green one with pink roses on the hemline. It's Bombay, after all. Everyone there is as stylish as they are here in Bangalore. Maybe even more. I'll take a few more clothes and a spare nightie. Suppose they ask me to stay back? I am her mother and she wants me. She needs me. Even now, as an adult, she asked for me. Imagine, a grown daughter. Hope she's more like me than that colourless Gopala.

Gracy was smiling to herself as she came out of the room. Gopala saw a middle-aged woman with thinning hair. He remembered the black tresses she would toss back when she knew he was watching. Now her waist was gone and she had covered her girth with a fossilized outfit which would have seemed appropriate in a nineties' potboiler. She was still caught in her youth and its dreams that to the young seem chaseable, findable and storable. Chasing dreams requires foolishness, stubbornness and belief. To look Gopala in the eye and talk to him Gracy must believe in the life she had chosen to lead.

Gopala tried not to stare. On one level, he respected her uninhibited air. On another, he was painfully aware that he could not be like her. He had been so careful all his life that he had never even got on a bicycle for the fear of falling. He did not want to risk an injury to learn to ride it. The only stressful rite of passage he went through was caring for Mynah and growing old while doing so.

Parents age in dog years while ensuring their wards grow and prosper. Gracy hadn't. She was as caught in her twenties as Gopala had been in hers. He was glad he came.

He checked out the sitting room and saw cushion covers embroidered by hand the way his mother used to. The side table was covered with another embroidered runner. The applique reminded him of his visits to relatives years ago. Clearly, Gracy did not get many visitors. She had no need for them.

She must spend her days waiting for Kalyan to come home to her. She must cook for him and ask about his day and then undress for him and then dress to please him. They must go out of town on trips and check into hotels as a couple.

Gopala imagined the scenario and smiled internally as he could not imagine her ticking the 'married' box on any registration book while doing so. That little detail meant exactly that to her—a little detail. He was sure that women ignored her and she smiled at one and all. Men must have tried their luck and some would have succeeded in winning a temporary and convenient place in her life. She must have spent hours alone, but was not lonely. Gracy was like that. She was complete in herself. She had managed what few do or can do. She had done justice to her existence.

They were seated in the airport lounge with an hour to go for their flight. Gopala looked at the plump stranger next to him and asked a question he had always wanted to.

'May I ask you a question, if you don't mind? Please don't mind.'

She turned her head at a confident angle that allowed her curls to fall on her face, only so that she could push them back.

'What is it, Gopala? Feel free to ask. We are old friends and meeting after so many years,' she said with warmth.

He wanted to get up and leave but instead found himself asking, 'Why did you and Hemanth break up?'

She laughed and said, 'Kalyan and I were friends at school. He was a toddy tapper's son. His family was poor. Hemanth was his brother, two years younger than him. Both brothers wanted me. But Hemanth told me he loved me first and we got very close. Kalyan was heartbroken. He told me much later that he had always been in love with me. That was after I moved into Hemanth's flat.'

Gracy grimaced and said, 'It was so tiny, Gopala. The front room was the size of my parents' scullery. The flat was in BTM Layout, quite close to your house in Jayanagar. No one but Kalyan visited us to show his support. That's what he told us. It was just a ruse, of course. He wanted to see me. No one else visited me there.

'My dear Gopala, as I wrote in that letter I left behind, I really liked you. You are a very nice man. But my heart was not in a humdrum marriage. I was trying very hard to be happy with you and trying to make my parents happy and all the relatives ecstatic and the villagers delirious with joy when I myself was so miserable. Then I met Hemanth again and those feelings I thought I had managed to forget rushed back. In any case, I would have left sooner or later, for living in that house and pretending to be happy would have made me feel suffocated after a while.'

Gracy ran her fingers through her hair and continued, 'Kalyan had been married for years before I moved in with Hemanth but he never got his wife to the flat. I still haven't met her. He does not speak of her much. I think soon after she found out about us, she left with their children for her parents' place. He was very disturbed about it. But he was back to his normal self in a few days as her parents sent her right back, saying she belonged with her husband. See, that's what parents are, Gopala. They are selfish cowards. For all the love and affection they profess for their children, they treat them like currency that must be invested and grown. I was paraded all the time by mine. Gracy, sing that hymn. Gracy, show those dance steps. Gracy got ninety-one in mathematics. Do you understand, Gopala, how horrendous parents can be?'

Gopala understood and made his peace with Gracy who had gotten glassy-eyed and comfortable in the rewind mode.

'Once Kalyan visited me when Hemanth was at work and then again the next day and soon he was coming home every afternoon. We got close. I always think of it as destiny. That Hemanth was my route to Kalyan.'

'How did Kalyan come into so much money that he could buy such a spacious flat for you?' asked Gopala, at ease now.

'He was a very good student. He studied ayurveda on a government scholarship, moved to Bangalore and rented a clinic. He somehow became an expert at solving back and joint problems with his oils and potions and earned a decent reputation. Over the years, he bought his own clinic, which grew into a hospital. Even foreigners began to visit. These days he says he is very grateful to computers and phones. Many of his patients are young executives with dislocated spines and swollen fingers and bulbous thumbs.'

Gracy smiled at Gopala, tilted her head a little like Mynah, and said, 'Back then, when I was with Hemanth, Kalyan would never visit me empty-handed. He was always gifting me things, something that Hemanth never did; flowers, earrings, chocolates. Not that I wanted gifts but the act showed that he wanted to please me. All Hemanth wanted was to marry me and he was confident that I wanted the same thing. But I kept postponing the date. If he spoke of January, I spoke of May, and if he spoke of May, I spoke of January. He began to fight with me all the time. This went on for two years. You know how our families live, Gopala. I was used to comfort... and his flat, his flat was just so tiny. Besides, as I was saying, he, I mean Hemanth, never did anything special for me unlike Kalyan. In any case, both brothers look a lot alike.'

Gopala grinned and said, 'How did Hemanth take to your new relationship?'

Gracy looked despondent. 'One day I decided enough was enough. I told him I wanted out. He was very nasty and called me a whore. He cut off ties with Kalyan too. People close to me do not understand me, Gopala. I am unlucky that way. You know, I did not attend my mother's funeral as my father found my number and called to warn me against stepping inside our home, saying you would be there with your family and that I was dead to him. In all these years that was the only time he spoke to me and that too with such cruelty. Others were permitted to see my dead mother but not I, their own daughter. They cut me off from their life because of a third party—you and your family. I brought them disrepute, it seems. But they broke my heart. I was their child. Not you.'

She stopped and smiled. 'But Kalyan has been very good to me, Gopala. No one has loved me the way he has. Thank god, I've been lucky as far as he is concerned.'

'What's his wife's equation with him?'

'Oh, that was an arranged marriage.'

The smell of spirit that defines airports and tries to pass off as freshener felt nauseating to Gopala.

❧

Mynah jumped at the ringing of the doorbell. Gopala had called her after landing.

Mynah stood behind Aruna as she unlatched the door. Gracy entered and looked past Aruna at the child born of her. Overcome with awe, she gazed at her for a few seconds and hugged her.

She is almost as beautiful as myself. Yes, I remember, she's got Gopala's yellow eyes. Actually, those eyes would look good on me. I could get lenses of that colour.

'Baby, I'm your amma,' she said.

The drama in Gracy's opening line was lost on a wounded Mynah who clung to her alien smell and cried quietly.

Gracy felt something she could not put a name to. She could not be detached. She looked up and met Aruna's blank countenance and Gopala's immersion in Mynah's breathing.

I should not have come.

Aruna fidgeted clumsily as Gopala cajoled Mynah to take a sip of water but the girl refused to let go of Gracy, who began to pat her and sob alongside for a lifetime of not knowing.

꧁

'Keep in touch, Mynah. Visit me when you are in Bangalore. You have my number now.'

'Okay, Mummy,' Mynah said truthfully. She could not bring herself to call her mother 'amma' as Gracy had addressed herself. Her mother was mummy to her. Even this woman was mummy to her.

'Bye,' said Gracy and turned before they could see her.

She was with them for three hours during which time Gopala recaptured Mynah's childhood, school and college years, friends, her job at the ad agency, her drive to rise in her career and win awards. When he spoke of her childhood friends, Mynah added Moltu's name. Gopala spoke of her colleagues and how supportive they were in her crisis as he brought up the topic that left a metallic taste in his mouth.

'Gracy, as I informed you, Mynah has recently broken up with her boyfriend.'

Mynah flared and said, 'I haven't. He has.'

Gracy pulled away from Mynah who was still clinging to her while both were seated on the divan. She laughed lightly and said, 'So God has given you another chance to find someone else. I would have been overjoyed.'

An angry Mynah retorted: 'Mummy, I'm not like you. Rohit should have been your son. He has blanked me out completely. I thought it was because of what Daddy said to him that day about his inheritance plan and all that, but now I believe he was just getting bored of me. Am I a toy? Do I have no value in anyone's life, except Daddy's? I'm only sure of one person in this world and that is him. Even Aruna aunty who is so protective of me might just blank me out tomorrow. Am I so easy to discard?'

Mynah bawled as she said this and Aruna rushed towards her. She kneeled on the floor, held her hands and said, 'Mynah, I will never leave you even if you do. You'll always be like my daughter. No, you will always be my daughter. I will formally adopt you, that is, if your father permits me to do so. I will speak to some lawyers about the process today itself. No one in their right mind can leave such a lovable child.'

Gracy glared at Aruna but chose to remain silent.

A sobbing Mynah said, 'But people who are supposed to be closest to me have left without looking back to check on me.'

Gopala got up and leaned against the window. Against the evening light, his figure looked like a cross between a saint and a ghost.

He chided Mynah: 'You've been close to all your friends,

Baby. Has anyone left you? Your mother did not even know you. You were only three months old and had no personality. All you did was cry, eat and sleep. If she had stayed on till you were a little older she would have never left. See this boy, this Rohit creature that's run away, comes across as totally self-involved and vile. I've told you so before. Now whether he is supremely successful or rich or brilliant or the best-looking man ever to set foot on this planet is immaterial. These are not virtues or signs of greatness. He is an ordinary boy who also seems like a skirt-chaser to me. We are better off without him. I agree, you've been unfortunate in two cases, in two primary relationships. But haven't you heard of the saying "third time lucky"?'

'How do you know, Daddy? The next man will also leave and the one after that.'

Mynah said this so despondently that Aruna grinned and said, 'You really believe that? Rohit is just so different from you. He is shallow and your father has rightly judged him as a ladies' man. I felt it too. You are his loss. He is nobody's loss. I think it's a blessing that you've been saved from being with him longer.'

'You both are just trying to make me feel better,' said Mynah sulkily.

Gopala replied, 'Mynah, you know I would never lie to you and Aruna aunty is like me.'

Mynah looked at Gopala with the faith of a believer.

She was drained and therefore lighter after the meltdown.

Gracy remained silent. In those hours of knowing from not, joining in Mynah's journey from a pup to her own person on the divan on which she was now seated with her shoulders hunched and hands between her thighs, Gracy aged. Her face sank into itself, the surround of her eyes grew crow feet, her lips drooped, her spine stooped neck down. She experienced the full force of the misery she had been subjected to, plucked as she was without preamble or warning from the cocoon drawn around her by Kalyan. Yes, when Gracy had left Mynah, she was a lump of needs and broad gestures. The girl sitting next to her, like herself in so many ways, left her immutably changed.

Gracy raged inside at her destiny, of being led like sheep, till she had chosen to take charge of herself. Now she was back to being carted around, this time to meet her child and face trial in a Bombay flat for a sin she had not committed. But her viscera thought otherwise. She had to speak up.

'Child, stop. I left not because I found you less lovable. I never wanted a child in the first place. I did not want to marry even. You were too little to feel real, as your father says, or I might have stayed back or taken you with me. I left after making sure you got breast milk for three months. I was not uncaring or callous. I did the best I could in the situation I found myself in. I had to go.'

Gopala offered a conciliatory smile to Gracy and genially blinked his eyes to assuage her. Aruna, who had no stake in Mynah's childhood, looked on aghast at what her runaway biological parent had said in her defence. Gopala met Aruna's eyes and she lowered them.

He walked up to Gracy and patted her shoulder.

'You poor girl. We don't hold you responsible. Those times were different. Knowing you, I wonder how your parents managed to get you into a wedding saree. You even smiled throughout the ceremony,' said Gopala to lighten the gathering.

Gracy teared again and said, 'They brainwashed me into thinking that our women never married anyone outside the community. They drilled it into my head that I would face unheard-of hardship with Hemant, and they were right about that. I thought I could make marriage work and mould myself into what was expected of me.'

Gopala took a deep breath and worded what he had wanted to ask for more than two decades, 'You never felt like visiting us?'

'Gopala, I was so happy to get away that the thought did not cross my mind. I knew you would take good care of Mynah, and your mother would take good care of you both.'

Mynah got up at that and with the fortitude of a person who has known love said, 'Thank you for coming, Mummy.

Chapter 23

Rohit plugged the pen drive and downloaded an Excel file for a terrace garden project in a Goregaon bungalow, not far from Malad. He called up the speciality soil contractor, gave him the specifics and leaned back in his chair. Unable to focus on the work at hand, he rang the real estate agent to inform him of his intention to move out of the flat and the locality. He wanted to shift to Bandra, the most sought-after suburb where the city's hippest lived their weekdays in smart formals and weekends in linen shorts, cool slippers and a carefree air.

As he ended the call, his face reddened. If it hadn't been for Gopala, he could have stayed on and not have had to move in the middle of the lease cycle. He would have weaned away from Mynah and shifted to Bandra as planned at his own pace and on his own terms.

The meddler.

Gopala had asked him point-blank, 'You want to marry Mynah?'

'It's too early in the day, sir,' Rohit had replied, seated opposite him in Aruna's flat.

'You have known her for a year. Isn't it time?' asked Gopala.

'I don't want to sound rude, sir, but it is our decision to make,' said Rohit in a staccato tone, the ends of his fingers twitching.

'She is in love with you. She called so excitedly to tell me about your relationship which she had managed to keep hidden for so long, I don't know how. Perhaps because you live in the same building. I immediately left for Mumbai on hearing of it. If you have a month or a year in mind, please share.'

'I still have a career to build, sir. My father has struggled very hard. It was very difficult for him to work and take tuitions with two children to feed and educate. I don't want the same situation for my family.'

'Mynah tells me you are well-placed. Besides, she will inherit our land. You don't have to worry about money.'

'Sir, I have no interest in OPM, Other People's Money,' Rohit said testily. 'Also, Mynah is too young. She has had very little exposure. I wish to wait at least two to three more years. There, you have the date.'

Gopala looked on with narrowed eyes. Celibacy had

compensated him with the power of dispassionate perception.

'She called to say she wanted to marry right away,' said Gopala with finality.

'She keeps saying that but you don't take her seriously, do you?' retorted Rohit.

'Rohit, the only person I have taken seriously for the past two decades is Mynah.' Gopala was unflinching and stoic.

'If my decision does not suit you, I'll stop seeing her. And, I repeat, I have no interest in your estate. You can keep it, sir,' declared Rohit and got up to leave.

'Is this a person in love talking?' asked Gopala evenly.

Rohit discounted Gopala's accusing import. He would not settle for or settle into anything. Prolonged intimacy bored him. He wanted physicality and the chase that ended in physicality. Mynah was all there always. Her indifference had evaporated the day he had stood outside her office to pick her up in the pouring rain without an umbrella.

'Rohit, what are you doing here?' she had asked, her eyes glistening with pleasure.

'Today's forecast predicted floods. When you left, I saw you did not have an umbrella or a windcheater on you. You usually return home by eight, so I thought I'll come by your office by six, in case you decide to leave early to dodge the rain. Should I call an Uber?'

Mynah grew wings at the obvious concern, blind to the obviousness of it.

Rashmi had been looking at Rohit for a few days and acting indifferent whenever he went up to her. He knew there was not much of a chase involved here, but the newness made him stretch and smile.

Chapter 24

VARUN, PAD AND RAKE VISITED MYNAH ON BEING GIVEN the go-ahead by Gopala over phone.

As they entered her room, Mynah's large eyes hurt them. Pad and Rake talked shop, amused her and announced that her idea for the commercial had passed muster.

'Really? That's so cool. Mangs had blocked this one too, right? He's been blocking every idea of mine. How did this miracle take place?' asked Mynah, perking up and smiling broadly.

'The other ideas were worse,' said Rake.

Mynah laughed. They were lying but they thought of dealing with truth later.

Ten days later, five suitcases arrived. Aruna got a new wardrobe installed in Mynah's room. Gopala arranged his clothes and shoes in it. Ramya the cook and Susheela did not get on too well, so Gopala packed her off to Bangalore. The driver had to leave for he was Ramya's husband and

Gopala would not separate a couple.

Gopala drove Mynah to Dr Radhakrishnan for her next appointment, this time to ask if she could resume work. Right through the half-hour journey, from the narrow bylane to the wide main road and the flyover, down on to the main road again and then the narrow streets of Fort, Mynah wished it was Rohit in the driver's seat. If it were him, she would have turned up the music and rolled down the window to let the wind abuse her hair and make them knotty. She would have reached out and felt the softness of his skin and he would have smiled back sweetly.

'I don't remember what you looked like the first time I saw you in the elevator,' she told Rohit, leaning against him on the bean bag in the hall of his flat.

He could only word an 'ouch' at her dismissal of their first encounter.

It was the morning after he had picked her up during the downpour. Mynah had called Rohit while still in that psychedelic stage between sleeping and waking, and offered to visit him at his upstairs flat. She had hugged him on entering and he had led her to the bean bag, hand on her waist, and slid next to her.

Mynah had offered him a conciliatory smile and said, 'Now I can't seem to remember anything else.'

She had wound her fingers in Rohit's hair and pulled him to her. She did not know that for Rohit, flushed in his victory and gifting generous kisses to the girl who was now completely his, the countdown had begun.

※

'Madam, Rohit is moving out. A tempo is parked in the porch,' Susheela whispered in Aruna's ear.

'Best news ever,' said Aruna and gave her a thumbs-up.

Mynah was watching a rom-com and feeling low about her freshly minted singleton situation.

Will I ever get a man again? Who will fall for me? Will I ever fall for a man? Am I capable of loving anyone as much?

Aruna told Mynah. Her face scrunched in response and she wept for hope vapourised.

Aruna stood where she was, powerless as Mynah faced rejection in its pervasive, corrosive magnitude and bottomed out. Broken people speak a customised silent dialect. They communicate by showing each other their wounds and watch the scabs form, one cell at a time.

That evening when Gopala was out for his evening walk, Aruna sat Mynah down and said, 'Baby, I think this Rohit is not as callous as I thought he was. He has some shame—I will not make the mistake of calling it honour—or he would have stayed on. I spoke to our wing's morning watchman and he said he had heard from someone that Rohit was moving to Bandra. So he has quit the locality too. He does not want to see you, which means you matter to him.'

'Aunty, you expect me to feel happy about this? That he does not want to see me again? Ever? He does not want to see me. That's the reality. The only reality.'

'No, it is not. His shift is a compliment to you. You are so important to him that he has fled, tail between his legs.'

Mynah got up and saw a pair of pigeons making out on the ledge of the window. Not wishing to scare away the fortunate lovers, she sat back down. Aruna suggested they go out for a walk. Mynah refused and retired to her room. As she lay staring at the ceiling fan whose rotation made its blades disappear, her phone rang. Although her heart had been subjected to continual sinking, it refused to learn from it and chose to sink yet again on seeing the caller was not Rohit.

'Hello, Varun,' she mouthed lifelessly into the phone, the disappointment in her voice palpable.

'Hey, Mynah. So you resume tomorrow, right? Pad told me. Do you want me to pick you up?'

'Daddy will drop me and he will sit in the lobby till I finish work.'

'Okay. Whatever you think works best,' he said and cut short the call, elated at the thought of seeing her in person in less than twenty-four hours.

Chapter 25

Rₒₕᵢₜ HAD MOVED INTO JAMUNA HEIGHTS FOR THE central address. His years in Dahisar had taught him that location counted. His classmates at LS Raheja School of Architecture in Bandra would sympathetically ask him whether his travel all the way from Dahisar tired him. He hated them for making it sound as if he trudged from Mars daily, and vowed to get out of his neighbourhood.

His father's move to Kalina in Santacruz was as much an outcome of his prodding as Radha's. A forty-two-year-old Ram took a home loan at ten per cent interest rate for a twenty-five-year tenure to afford the two-bedroom flat. A home that Rohit left a year into his job with a second-rung architecture consultation firm that specialized in landscaping for public spaces and developers, an area that appealed to him.

A keen painter, Rohit fit right in, in the artistically evolved Lalbaug.

His Kalina home was filled with canvases of nature copied from Monet, Homer and Van Gogh. He did some original work using photographs of naked women and others in varied stages of undress. His parents did not stop him from pursuing his hobby. The one time he was forced to hide his nudes was when his relatives, those his mother hosted apropos their bank balance, came visiting. Radha's fawning over them made Rohit resolve to never be in his mother's position.

No relative of his was ever invited to his Lalbaug flat where he laid out the nudes in the hall for the man servant to see and appreciate.

Rohit took the keys and gave the flat a glance-over for anything left behind, banged the door shut and left.

His mind wandered Mynah's way when he got into the elevator and liftman Raja smiled at him toothily, attempting to share in his masculine glory of being an invader and abandoner. Rohit glared at him for he would no longer need him, the aggression destroying the momentary bonhomie that Raja had wished to transmit to an openly hierarchical man.

Raja had not known that he would end up as a liftman, an aspirational post among his lot, when one of his daily labourer parents had bludgeoned the other with a blunt hammer. He was nine then, a Class III student of a school run by the municipal corporation that gave him free food which he and his friends gobbled without tasting. He had returned from school that day to his shanty in a large eastern slum pocket of Kurla, and felt obvious relief on seeing his father's pulped body. He had exchanged smiles with his mother and two siblings who had blissfully told him of the fight that had led to the permanent ouster of Pramod from the world. Pramila, his mother, nee Sushma and renamed by her in-laws to match her husband's name as was customary, had been quickly arrested. She had steadfastly denied having killed her husband despite being herself pulped to near-death in police custody. Her children had wailed outside and consistently corroborated their mother's claim. She was let off after three years as there was no eyewitness to the crime and all evidence was meticulously wiped off by her industrious children.

During Sushma's absence, Raja had to drop out of school and work in a garage. His sister Tina and brother Dharmendra, both older than him and both named after movie stars Pramod adored, had insisted that he contribute to the family income and not waste time at school. Tina and Dharmendra worked as sorters with a diamond merchant at Opera House, a glitzy hub of dealers in gold and precious stones to the south. The siblings' work hours were spent peering at carbon rocks pinched between tweezers and held under magnifying glasses to ascertain their value. Raja was too young to be anyone other than a sooty helper at a used cars garage. He was underpaid for years but his felicity for flashing his teeth and kowtowing landed him a liftman's job in a Kurla building when his face grew a moustache. Within months, he got his big break with a premium housing society maintenance and security agency. He was placed some years hence in this gated complex at Lalbaug.

Raja did get job satisfaction. The initial nausea of constant movement in elevators, not dissimilar to what newly recruited aircraft crew must experience on takeoff and landing, was gone and he enjoyed ferrying all kinds of people and listening on. The pay was good enough to merit a wife, a son and two sonography sessions to abort two female foetuses.

As Rohit slowly moved his disgusted eyes away from Raja after establishing his superiority, he hoped the elevator would not stop on the fourth floor. He was done with the irritating tragedy slung on him by that underdeveloped weakling of a girl.

He had recoiled from her on noticing a weakness the first

time, a shortcoming that could not be brushed off with a generous smile.

'If you wish to do well in life, you have to do what you love. You have to give it your one hundred per cent. There are no half measures. Burn the midnight oil, strain your eyes, tire out your muscles, go without food, sleep, do whatever it takes but hit the goalpost. You just have to keep trying till you get whatever it is that you set out to achieve, whether it is an education or a job. Once you get that dream job, you must strive to excel in it. Money, recognition, fame will follow. They have to. They have no choice,' he had told Mynah agitatedly on hearing that she had entered advertising as she did not get a job as a journalist.

Myah had replied, 'But, Rohit, I got into journalism itself because I did not get admission into a law college. Two of my closest friends from school did and I was so disappointed that I didn't, as I could not hang out with them anymore. I thought then why not try journalism as the aptitude tests at school had spotted that I could write. Besides, the institute was very close to my place. Why not give it shot, I thought.'

Rohit had found it difficult to focus on what she was spouting. People who floated, who had no direction, did not deserve his mind space.

He wanted a woman as driven as himself. Not a child who went with the flow. He wanted a partner to reach someplace with and then do a high-five with. She had to be a player. A woman who knew the score. Not one who kept it. A woman who could sense a move before it was made. Mynah would not know that a move had been made in the first place.

He was greatly relieved when the dalliance was over. Gopala, the holier-than-thou father of the dimwit girl, had gifted him a respectable exit. Wounded pride is a legitimate reason to bolt.

Chapter 26

I N A CHAUFFEUR-DRIVEN CAR, NAVIGATING THE TRAFFIC
somewhere near Jamuna Heights sat Subodh, browsing
financial news on his phone. He was not a news buff but
now read up to dazzle Harsha and her friends who had
received expensive education, unlike him.

But Subodh struggled to stay abreast of contemporary
affairs to regurgitate at social do's to get and keep Harsha
in a good mood. They did two a week, sometimes more.
All left him winded. He was thrown by the alpha charge at
these events filled with the uber successful. When Subodh
was articulate, he was out-articulated. If he voiced an opinion
that countered the popular view, he was quietly put in his
place with patient smiles. The uber successful were gentle
with him and distant, and remained so. Subodh thought
they were removed since he was a mere corporate executive
and they were industrialists and owners of institutions. He
suspected that some of their businesses had gone bust but
that did not prevent him from shrinking in front of even
those assumed bankrupt.

Perhaps if Subodh had said he did not have an opinion or care to have one, he might have earned a genuine smile. Sometimes Harsha would join the other side and rib him for some good-natured fun.

Subodh felt like a dog on a leash, the way his former wife had felt with him, or maybe she hadn't. He did not think of Aruna. The bond had dissolved for him the day the doctor had laughed at his sperm count. Subodh had blanked out that interaction as well. The uncomplaining Aruna was a non-person who must be remembered and visited to be given the news of his brother's death as it was the right thing to do.

Chapter 27

'ONE, TWO, THREE, RUN TO ME.' SUBODH'S MOTHER spread her arms and watched him bound up to her, gurgling and rolling. When he was within reach, she clasped him to her chest and kissed him. Prerna could not have enough of her three-year-old second son. The older one, Vinod, was ten and had no time for her. Subodh followed her around loyally, like a textbook toddler. His mother was his hero.

His father had died when Subodh was young. He was just a year old then, like Harsha when her father had died.

A large, framed touched-up photograph of Subodh's father hung in the family's front room, the way the departed are remembered in homey households. The garland of plastic mogra flowers strung neatly around the photo frame had been thoughtfully bought at the Lalbaug market by a relative. When Subodh was a little older, he noticed his good-looking father's stained teeth and crooked grin in the blown-up photograph. When he overheard his mother speak of his womanising misadventures to her sister, Pari, he came to associate bad teeth with debauchery and ensured his own were forever taken care of.

One episode marked him. His father's last girlfriend who had also been his colleague, Hima, had landed at their residence days after his death, ostensibly to seek refuge with Prerna, to cling to the one person she assumed was closest to her departed lover. Prerna had recalled the event, for it was nothing short of an event, in front of Pari in the kitchen that day and both had collapsed on the floor with uncontrollable laughter. Subodh had giggled along in a corner, unnoticed.

Prerna had beaten Hima with an heirloom lathi right uptil the compound of their building complex in the salubrious Gamdevi of south Mumbai where Mahatma Gandhi's home peacefully stands. The neighbours thoroughly enjoyed the sight of a new widow in a white saree striking a young girl in a white salwar kameez like a warrior queen. When Prerna called her a whore, some encouraged her to hit her on the head and finish the husband-snatcher for good. Prerna was upset at being left a widow at thirty with two children to raise. The wrenching reality of having to run around for their vaccinations, clothes, school meetings and covering mountains of school books with brown paper by herself year on year was unbearable.

Subodh had wanted to see Hima since the day he had been

an onlooker to the hilarious conversation between his mother and aunt. His entire life Subodh kept an eye out for the imaginary creature that had taken form in his head, more so in his colleagues as she had been his father's, and more so after his confidence in his manliness was shaken.

Harsha was not a colleague but with her he felt alive again. He stopped flirting with other women, colleagues or otherwise, as he was frightened of losing her. He was caught in an unfamiliar territory, wanting to ride Harsha's world that he thought of as on a higher plane than his. But in his struggle to feel potent all he managed to do was to turn himself into passable arm candy.

Chapter 28

THE TAWNY-EYED MYNAH, LIKE THE YELLOW-EYED *peetanetra* bird, was up early. Rake had warned her if she did not turn up at work that day, she would have to pass up the 360-degree campaign. It was a threat that worked. A threat he made because how could he not. It was more than forty days since she had disappeared and he wanted to kill Rohit, whoever he was, for keeping her chirpy presence off the office floor.

When she had not turned up for two days without notice, Rake had called her and then asked Varun, 'I always thought you had a thing for her. How did you let that fellow snatch her?'

Varun had shrugged helplessly and said he was going for a walk.

Rake was hopeful that Mynah would hook up with Varun on the rebound. It would help her case and stop interfering with his own mental peace.

🌱

Gopala drove her to work and settled himself in the office lobby to wait it out for her till evening. He did not want to step out, even to the washroom, in case Mynah came charging out in agony. With that in mind, he had packed a cucumber, tomato and cheese sandwich. He wanted to be present to scoop her up and take her home if need be.

As Mynah stepped into the office, her team surrounded and hugged her in turns. She began to shiver and look for a dark corner to hide. Varun did not hug her like the rest though. He did something that came naturally to him. He unselfconsciously kissed her forehead and led her to her desk, her hand firmly in his. They circled their rounded, pod-like departmental separation from the client servicing department, to enter the narrow opening to their work area. In some strands of Indian mythology, when a man and a woman hold each other's right hands, they are considered as good as married. These two had even circled the department to enter it while holding hands, the way it is done in wedding halls to formalize a marriage, but seven times and in front of the Fire God as witness. In those seemingly mundane moments Mynah broke the jinx associated with her name. She was not alone in the wood and glass office, and that could be said with certitude, like a hot wax seal on a signed and dated stamp paper.

Varun had pretended not to hear her when Mynah first brought up Rohit days after the rainy interlude. He tried to look through her, an indifference that Mynah did not even register. She began to pour out what she called her love story as if he were a sponge. He was forced to be all ears. The pain of listening, of pretending to be indifferent to her and her attachment to an attractive man ceaselessly cut him. It was a wound not allowed to heal, for Varun would look forward to seeing her and hearing her voice the next weekday, even if all she spoke of was Rohit.

When she did not turn up at work the day Rohit stopped taking her calls, Varun dialled her and shot off a message on WhatsApp. He waited for her response that did not come despite the blue double ticks that declared the message had been seen.

When Mynah did not take his calls for two days, he gave himself a week and dialled again. She cut the call. He fell back into his seat. He did not call again and listless days lengthened into weeks. When Rake and Pad pointedly told him of their plan to call on her and asked whether he would like to join them, he shrugged a 'yes'. They would not have accepted a 'no'. He would not have said it either.

After he landed at Mynah's residence with the two, he stood back to keep Mynah from seeing his face and did not speak a word. He just nodded before leaving. The next day though he took advantage of the fresh opening and called her. She picked up. He began to call her every evening after work and she began to pick up the phone to continue speaking of Rohit *ad nauseam*. An elated Varun listened on, hoping against fragile hope that the bastard would not make a reappearance. By being a genuinely good listener, that endangered species, Varun managed to make her wait for his calls, if only to vent and release, and turned himself into a habit, for he was determined, dogged, patient and wily, like his father, Bob.

Bob had trudged with his family from Sialkot of the newly divided state of Punjab up north to the Bombay of 1947, when portions of north-western and eastern India were ripped without anaesthesia and declared a separate nation of Pakistan as India painfully gained its independence from the British Raj. Countless people were forced to choose sides and switch homes on the sole ground of religion.

Mass voluntary and involuntary migrations across millennia—lugging of homes, histories, life patterns and habits from place to place—are the end product of belief in a singular concept that is effectively presented as the only way. All are expected to follow its lead, voices on mute, souls benched.

Varun's grandfather, Giridharilal, left behind a western menswear business to travel thousands of kilometres from his magnificent residence that boasted twenty rooms and a dining table with twenty gold and blue velvet chairs. Twenty was the family's lucky number, an astrologer had assured him.

When Giridharilal shut his eyes afterwards he saw the impressive porch of his home held up by stone columns and caught a glimpse of his sprightly shoes on the outdoor floor panelled with polished Burma teak slabs when he left for work. The textured, lightly sloping lawn in front had a pool with a marble fountain at its centre which spouted water from an urn held by a semi-clothed sculpture of a rotund woman. His wife, two unmarried daughters, four sons and their three wives would swim in the pool on summer afternoons before tea time.

Their days would begin with echoes of prayers that travelled from a cathedral nearly a kilometre away. Bob's family knew the prayers by heart and remembered to thank the Lord along with those gathered inside the holy structure's stone walls.

⁂

Giridharilal had impotently crumpled the ten hundred-rupee notes in his left shirt pocket that he had hastily snatched from the family locker while leaving for Bombay, after locking the door with a robust bronze lock and pulling it to see if it would come off. When it did not, he had broken down, not caring for the devastating impact of the crumbling of the patriarch on his family. They left for the railway station on three tongas with some money, some lighter zari sarees, sherwanis and men's suits stuffed inside trunks. The jewellery was sewn inside vests that the men wore under their shirts.

The family survived the journey through strange lands, by train and road, dazed and constipated, for they could not bring themselves to eat menial food and that too without cutlery or being waited upon by staff, or use public toilets so filthy that no description could capture what they had seen.

Caught in the nightmare of dislocation, they would now be refugees and be reduced to statistics, to approximate numbers.

Giridharilal and his brood had boarded the tongas arranged by a neighbour who had whispered urgently that a murderous mob was on its way. Riots had broken out all over following the country's mutation—the victims' revenge on themselves.

No one came. The looting happened over weeks, a few knick-knacks and furniture at a time, mostly picked when no one was watching. The family heard of the silent carnage months later from a few of Giridharilal's friends who had chosen to stay behind and sit it out till anger ebbed. They were wiser, or perhaps fortunate, to have stayed on and survived in safe houses, for violence like serenity is a phase. Both anger and calm need fuel and fuel has a lifespan.

✿

Giridharilal died within a year of reaching Bombay, his migrant self dwarfed into nihilism.

Varun's father Bob—European names were in fashion then—was the youngest at seven when his family was uprooted. He vowed to get out of the refugee camp for the Partition-displaced in Bombay where his family had landed and was forced to coop into for two decades. He hated his days in their two-room tenement in the eastern Chembur suburb for as long as he lived there.

He went to a night school for impoverished students where he would lie to his classmates about his riches and boast about his bungalow to all. None of his friends was invited home: none believed him, none teased him. All, barring none, acted adequately impressed, but Bob did not see through their empathetic subterfuge because for him his story was not a lie. He was living his future already.

Bob, who had been accidently conceived when his parents were ready to start looking for marital matches for their children, was the first to wriggle out of the tenement after he began to make decent money as a real estate broker. He also decided it was time to leave the family's struggling business of trading in menswear in their new city.

He rented a room in one of the Art Deco buildings along Marine Drive, though not a sea-facing one. The flat was owned by an eighty-three-year-old childless widow whose wealthy relatives had no interest in her or her wealth. She died four years after Bob moved in, leaving the flat to him as a reward for his charm and attentions. When he learnt of the inheritance, he whooped, laughed and kissed the lawyer who had broken the news to him and who did not kiss him back or smile. Within a week he sold the flat, added his own savings to the kitty and bought a three-bedroom apartment in another building along the same row. This one too did not face the sea. Bob hated the blinding sea that threw up the blinding glare of the sun. He pined for an independent house with a lawn but did not want to settle for one in a far-off suburb. Working out a compromise, he built a little fountain in the middle of his spacious living room. When he called his aged family to his young home for the housewarming, they prayed for permanent prosperity, bounty and blessings for their baby brother while silently gazing at a familiar-looking white lady pouring out an uninterrupted supply of water from a pot into a miniature pool in the middle of the room.

Chapter 29

Bob and his much-younger wife Uma—he married after his fiftieth birthday—wanted their children, Varun and Nisha, to join professional courses. All his life Bob felt mournful while passing a college, for he had been too immersed in the practicalities of building a lost world outside educational institutions to seek admission into one. Colleges, to him, were places that carried the promise of respect from erudite society. He was seen as an uncouth broker. His clients did not value his opinion on anything other than real estate. That hurt.

He forced both his children to study engineering.

Varun left Bob devastated by not cashing in on his degree in electronic engineering he earned by studying at the same institute as Nisha. But then his son got two back-to-back promotions at the ad agency he had steadfastly chosen to work in, in spite of Bob's blood-curdling threats. When Varun's team won an award in the third year of his joining the agency, Bob allowed himself to feel pride in his son and not just relief at his having taken up a job and sticking to it.

Chapter 30

I**T WAS MYNAH'S THIRD DAY AT WORK POST THE APOCALYPSE** in her adult, sentient life. To keep her busy, Rake dumped clerical work on her such as filling up time sheets which she had neglected to do for a couple of months. He also steadfastly refused to engage with her about the campaign she was to have bagged by citing a vague deadline.

Varun gave her a bar of dark chocolate every day, the way he had done the first two days of her return since he had read somewhere that it was a mood elevator. She accepted it with a polite thank you, barely noticing the gesture, though on some level expecting it out of a quickly formed habit. Years later, for time as we know it is constant in its linear trajectory, she would feel her throat tighten at the memory that required no filter. She would bow to it in gratitude, hands folded and eyes shut to not allow it to slip out of the lids.

Chapter 31

P EOPLE MOVE AND THE MOVEMENT SETS OFF A CHAIN OF
seismic ripples. If they must reset their lives, so must the
addresses they have left behind, passed through and reached.
The swell of newness must be accepted till it wears off and
gets less new. Infinite ripples created by the mobile crest
and ebb in a cosmic dance that can be understood and
interpreted only in hindsight, for one must turn back to
look at it. It cannot be seen upfront.

Mynah laughed with less abandon but laugh she did. The
broken parts of a forgotten Moltu cried themselves to sleep
in their empty Bangalore room. Gopala had no furniture to
wipe nor did he need a mobile network to follow Mynah in
Mumbai, a city he no longer associated with bomb blasts,
having made it his home. His relatives back home in Bangalore
passed his shut Jayanagar home and discussed the price it
would fetch. Gopala himself was not averse to the idea of
selling it and buying a flat in Lalbaug. Aruna who had been

in Lalbaug for a while was left with a wispy recall of her life before Mynah. Her relatives, friends and former neighbours at her birthplace of Pune and Prabhadevi in Mumbai where she had lived earlier with Subodh discussed her with a warmth that kept growing as they imagined her as more beautiful and more accommodating than she had been. For in nostalgia, everything is more beautiful. Aruna had no knowledge of the growing appreciation of her absentee beauty, and if she had, it would have made her smile distractedly, that's about it. She sold the Pune flat, with Suyash's blessings and signature, to a young family that infused the place with its energy, wiping her school teacher parents' history. Suyash was sent half the proceeds of the sale and he in turn sent Aruna the two-word acknowledgement with a smiley. The message felt cold and reminded her of Harsha's look when she had entered her home with Subodh the first time.

Unknown to her, Harsha's eyes did have it in them to sparkle when she interacted with her friends from school. The girls, now middle-aged women, met up from wherever they were for the big days a few times a year and shared regular and irregular happenings in their lives, shed a few tears and laughed a considerable amount. A temporarily rejuvenated and receptive Harsha would smile with her eyes often, till the halo faded.

But Bob had begun to smile all the time at neighbours he bumped into after shutting the door to his flat with its constantly flowing water. He carried the confidence of a man who had done something right. He heard that the family home in Sialkot which he left behind as a child had been converted into a government building. The long dried-up fountain had been razed and a portion of the plot where the lawn had been left to weed was concretized to serve as a public parking lot. He was glad to hear that no family had usurped the building and he feverishly believed that no one had taken a dip in his pool before it was filled up.

Bob's son and Mynah began to see each other outside work. She comfortable in his company and he glad for hers. But Mynah's mother returned to Bangalore flustered and began to have unpleasant dreams, one of which made her call Kalyan one early morning. He rushed to hold her till she felt safe again, after feigning an emergency to his wife, Moni, who had sat up next to him on hearing the sound of the phone at an ungodly hour. She heard every word Gracy tearfully uttered in the quiet and kicked Kalyan out of bed with her betrayed legs for he had looked her in the eye and said what he said. She screamed and asked him whose back was broken at this time of the day and then turned her own back at him. Before shutting the bedroom door, Kalyan had looked at Moni with tenderness, some of it scooped out of his quota for Gracy who kept seeing Mynah's yellow eyes before opening hers.

Epilogue

Mynah was roused by her phone alarm, a mellow ringtone of harps and chirping birds. She remembered it was Sunday, the brightest day of the week, and that she had a movie to catch with Daddy and Aunty. She checked her phone and there was a 'good morning' WhatsApp message from Varun. If there hadn't been one, she would not have absent-mindedly nodded at her phone and her brow might have furrowed. She went to the hall and opened the window to let in the morning air. The tall gulmohar outside had broken into its annual rash of blood-red flowers. Grey pigeons, white doves, a few that looked like both, parakeets, sunbirds, a bulbul and some mynahs were resting in the tree's shade on its higher, cooler branches. The entire batch flew out haphazardly when a firecracker burst, for it was only eight in the morning and the birds did not wish to dance to drums and shehnai that a boisterous human wedding party had begun to play at full blast in the compound below.

Mynah looked down to see the wedding party with its unmistakable groom in a sequined maroon kurta and cream churidar teamed with a pair of golden mojaris on his feet. His face would have been hidden completely by a curtain of white jasmine strands tied to his gold and orange turban, had he not lifted the floral veil with an elbow while dancing. His uninhibited moves made Mynah laugh out so loud that her voice carried over the music. The groom lifted the veil higher, shaded his vision with the other hand and gave a thumbs-up to Mynah on spotting her while continuing to gyrate. She threw him a flying kiss which he caught with the free hand.

As the party moved out of the gate, dancing and singing along with the instrumental band that played latest movie music, the birds made their way back to the tree.

Mynah took a deep breath and smelled the aroma of warm breakfast being cooked by Aruna. The door to the flat opened and Susheela walked in. She headed straight to the kitchen and excitedly told Aruna that Suraj had bought a first-hand bike and offered her a box of milky sweet barfi. A smiling Aruna entered the hall to share the good news with Gopala who was watching Mynah through a mist that had a place in summer.

Acknowledgements

Those who made it happen.

The late Darryl D'Monte, senior journalist and author, for his insights and the gift of his 2002 book *Ripping the Fabric: The Decline of Mumbai and its Mills*. Neera Adarkar and Meena Menon for their 2004 book *One Hundred Years, One Hundred Voices: The Millworkers of Girangaon. An Oral History*. Columbia Global Centers for hosting the 2017 exhibition 'Archiving the Mill Lands: The Mythologies of Mumbai Project'. Datta Iswalkar and Pravin Gagh of Girni Kamgar Sangharsha Samiti. Veteran journalist and friend Ambarish Mishra. Parag Chavan, Shiv Sena's deputy branch head, Sewri. Anurag Agnihotri, managing partner, India (West), Ogilvy, Mumbai. Bharat Gothoskar, founder and chief evangelist of Khaki Tours. Shaan Lalwani, a masters in Landscape Management from University of Sheffield (UK) and owner of Vriksha Nursery, Mumbai. Dr Ashit Sheth, honorary psychiatrist, Bombay Hospital. Dr Nandita Bose, my 'tough' editor. Rashmi Menon, managing editor, Amaryllis, for her trust. My family for being my family. My friend and lifeboat Shinie Antony, the kickass author-editor.

www.ingramcontent.com/pod-product-compliance
Lightning Source LLC
Chambersburg PA
CBHW031952010726
47493CB00007B/2178